MAXINE

A NOVEL BY KATIE CORD

Michela,
Puberty is hell.
Glad you made it!
♡, Katie C~

Dedicated to all who've ever felt like a freak.

You are one of many in an army of misfits.

Solidarity. Always.

Hurrah.

Rothgen Depends on Our Girls!

To be a good female citizen, you must always be your best. It is your duty from preschool onward to eat right, listen to your parents, and always follow the rules of the Rothgen Corporation. You must exercise, have proper hygiene, and keep the items provided for you neat and tidy. Make an effort to be your most attractive, friendly, and smart self. Rothgen boys need healthy balanced girls to interact with so they can grow up to be our next leaders. If the boys are provided girls that are unkempt, sassy, or no fun to talk to, our society will suffer. Remember girls: boys want perfection.

Never forget that without your cooperation, our way of life would end. We need young women who can keep our young men on the right direction for success.

–excerpt from *The Rothgen Guide to Being a Young Woman*

CHAPTER 1

"Penn, I don't know what you're doing, but seriously, you are making me sick with how much better you look than me!" Karlene Indiana said as she brushed her long, mousy brown hair.

"Karly, stop it," Ellen Pennsylvania said. She pulled her knee-high sock up, then folded it down. She paused, looking down at the shiny concrete floor.

She wasn't even sure why her skin was glowing brighter than normal, her hair was thicker, her nails longer, and her waist tapered in over the past weekend, giving her the perfect hourglass figure.

She slipped her oxfords on, trying to forget. She didn't like focusing on her looks like Karlene, Marie, and Esther.

"I'm just saying. If you get any prettier, you'll be as big a freak as Mess-a-shit-etts over there." Karlene tilted her head towards a chubby shy girl who had stringy black hair. Ellen looked up to see the girl gawking at her.

"Hey perv, quit staring!" Karlene yelled.

"Gawd, I hate gym," Marie said as she walked around the lockers in just her bra and panties. She squinted at Ellen. *There is something wrong with her. I just don't know what it is*, she thought. *Being pretty shouldn't freak everyone out this much.*

As Ellen leaned down to tie her shoes, her world spun. She grasped the bench she'd been sitting on. "Whoa. I don't feel so good." She stood up and leaned on the lockers.

"Penn, do you want to go to the nurse?"

Ellen nodded.

"We don't know what happened, but Ellen doesn't feel good," Karlene said to the school

2

nurse.

The stout, plain-faced nurse looked Ellen up and down. Then she turned back to her typewriter.

"Lay her over there, and then you're excused." The nurse continued to type. The girls assisted Ellen over to the medical cot.

"Can we wait with her? *Please*?" Marie begged.

"No. Now go." The nurse glared at the girls.

The girls backed out of the office slowly, looking at one another as they went. They weren't used to the nurse acting like this.

"Shut the door behind you."

The girls obliged as they gave each other worried looks.

The nurse swiveled her chair around, stood, and strode over to Ellen. She looked down at her and shook her head. "We had high hopes for you, kiddo."

Ellen groaned.

The nurse grabbed the phone and spoke into it without dialing, her voice low. "Ellen Pennsylvania is done." She hung up the phone, proceeded to her locked cabinet, and pulled out a pre-filled syringe.

Ellen rolled over and looked at her. "What're you doing?"

"Oh sweet girl. At least you got to be pretty."

The nurse leaned over and injected Ellen in the arm.

HAPPY BIRTHDAY

In the course of every young woman's life, there comes a day when she judges her worth by the size of her breasts. That day had come for Maxine Massachusetts, and it made her feel like shit. It had started in the girls' locker room yesterday, and now preoccupied her.

She'd watched the other girls in various stages of undress, some totally bare-chested, with round mounds that would overflow a hand if cupped. Others were small, but raised away from the chest wall enough to look like boobs. Esther Hampshire had long, large nipples that drooped like the shoulders of a defeated athlete.

Maxine had looked down at her own chest. Her breasts were unshaped; her nipples were inverted, and surrounded by small, purplish areolas. It was the start of a cascade of round, pasty fat that ended at her feet.

Today Max turned sixteen, and she felt like a freak.

She hadn't started her period, and still didn't need a bra unless her Mom caught her not wearing it. This was a big contention between the two; her mother thought it necessary that she "train" her nonexistent boobs. In Maxine's opinion, if there was nothing to train, then there was no reason to wear the horrible contraption.

Just in case her mother checked, Max grabbed the itchy polyester torture device out of her top dresser drawer. Her mother had shown her how to put the damned thing on properly, but Max didn't see the point. She pulled off her sweater and slid the bra over her head. For a moment, she entertained the idea of putting a sock in each cup to see if anyone would notice.

Then she thought about the "glowing girls," as she liked to call them, laughing at her for trying to pose as something she was not. Those girls could smell discomfort and fear. If Max forgot to wear deodorant, they somehow sensed her weakness, and ripped her apart.

When it had happened she'd gone into the girls' room, locked herself in a stall, and smelled her armpits. There'd been no smell. The glowing girls had just *known*.

Max shuddered as she slipped her sweater back over her head. At least she was a junior; the younger kids just ignored her. But the girls her own age targeted her, as though she were a freaky little monster sent to devour anything beautiful and bright. Max looked at the walls of her bedroom. *Beautiful and bright. Blah.*

The soft pink walls made her uncomfortable, and the pictures of flowers and young girls playing with a hula hoop in a field of daisies just seemed fake to her.

When she was younger, she had gone to the other girls' homes. Their bedrooms had all looked the same, even down to the white lace comforters on their beds. Max's Mom had turned in Max's first comforter when she was age ten, and Max had anticipated a different one, with bright purple flowers. Instead it was the same thing as before, only newer.

Everything in McCarthy is perfect, normal, and complete except me, Max thought as she slipped her shiny loafers on. Her house looked exactly like almost everyone else's house on her street.

There were exceptions—some of the families with more children had larger versions of her home—but they all looked the same. The homes were what had used to be called Craftsman style, with grey paint and white trim. The only thing the kids were allowed to choose was the colors of their clothes, and you could only get so much of each color a year.

Max loved black. It was the most intelligent choice. It hid dirt well, and most importantly, it was the only color that covered most of her flaws. Her mother had made her choose pink one year. It had been the worst feeling of her life. Pink brought out the paleness of her skin, its blue undertone, and the light grey rings under her eyes.

She'd felt like a lumpy piece of cotton candy tromping down the hallways. She didn't look like the other girls, and never would.

Max stood up from the full-sized bed and went over to her vanity mirror. She had learned to use talcum powder to dust around her eyes to make her skin tone look even and hide some of the blue veins that seemed to creep up her neck when she was exceptionally exhausted. Her mother had lied at the commissary and told them that her father needed the talcum powder for his feet, so that she could bring it home for Max's face.

That was one thing that Max's Mom did well: she twisted the truth to get what she needed. Her mother told her it was called survival, and that it was okay as long as no one got hurt in the process.

The girls were not supposed to wear makeup. Her mother called it her war paint, not makeup; Max needed war paint to endure high school. Her mother refused to talk about the things she'd done to stay alive. She only knew that her mother and father had met on the road: nothing more, nothing less.

"Max, do you think you might want to come down and eat breakfast before you go to school?" Max's mother yelled from downstairs. "Your hypoglycemia will get the best of you."

Her shoulders felt heavy. She'd stalled in her room for too long; she dreaded the spectacle her parents were going to put on for her birthday.

She was positive there were little handcrafted paper flowers on the dining room table, a bright, cheerful tablecloth, and some kind of breakfast concoction that her mother had put together using commissary items that other mothers might not have thought to combine.

She grabbed her school-issued backpack and slung it over her arm. The pack weighed at least thirty pounds, and only added to the burden of Max's one-hundred-and-eighty-five-pound frame.

Before she closed the door to her room, she checked that everything was in place. The white frilly comforter was laid out perfectly, all papers were organized neatly on her desk, and all her clothes were folded in the drawers of her dresser.

There were rumors that an official came through the houses and inspected everything while the kids attended school. It was hard for her to believe that anyone would check to see if she'd folded her underpants, but she wasn't willing to find out. She closed the door behind her. Even if she wanted to hide something, she didn't have anything to hide from her parents.

As she went down the stairs, a smile spread across her face; the smell of eggs, bacon, and batter floated in the air. Breakfast pizza. Maxine anticipated her birthday breakfast, but to her surprise, it wasn't there. Her backpack dropped to the floor.

"Mom, where are you?" Max asked.

"I'm in the kitchen. Where else would I be?" Maxine's Mom yelled. "Come in here and eat. You know you can't be late."

Disappointment passed through her as she walked to the kitchen. Her mother had not made a big deal about her birthday.

Erin Massachusetts turned away from the oven

to smile at her daughter. She had long, flowing, reddish-brown hair that was streaked with little silver highlights, and liked the bright and beautiful colors that turned Max away.

Today, she wore a pink button-up top that made her hair shine and the freckles on her nose pop out. Her crème-colored apron with deep pink roses complemented the shirt as though they were intentionally coordinated. Her body was fit and lean, like all women were required to be.

Maxine's Mom laughed sometimes about being a homemaker. Sometimes, the laugh was nervous; other times it sounded sad. She could never tell with her Mom.

Her mother set a plate on the island table; golden birthday pizza in the shape of a heart was placed in the middle of diced potatoes that had been fried to a crisp perfection.

"Happy birthday, sweetheart." Her mother came around the bar, giving Max a body-engulfing hug. Max felt reassured by the squeeze, but something inside her felt compelled to push her Mom away. She shrugged her mom off and sat down to eat.

"Thanks, Mom," mumbled Max.

"After school, I was thinking we could go to the commissary and use your birthday voucher," her mother said while wiping off the counter. "You shouldn't let it go to waste."

"Moooom, I hate the commissary. Everything there is so gross. You know the clothes there don't fit me." Max didn't want to discuss fashion with her Mom.

"Look, this is all we have," her mother said, looking at Max with impatience, "and if you'd try to exercise a little, the clothes would fit, and you'd feel better about wearing something besides black."

"Mom, I try, but my body won't change," Max said, looking down at her food. She mumbled under her breath, "I hate gym."

"As long as you keep trying, I know something will change. It has to. Every girl goes through a chubby stage," Erin said, rubbing Max's hair.

"Why can't I wear what will fit?" Max asked. All the kids knew her mother modified the clothes: extended waistbands, shirts with panels on the sides, and sweaters that were stretched to the seams.

"Mrs. Washington told me that she would love to do an exchange. Maybe I can trade her some clothes, so we can modify things for you."

She had to credit her mother: she knew how to work the system.

Max ate two bites. Then she held back, though she wanted to eat more. Her mother raised an eyebrow at the small amount Max consumed. Max gave her a challenging look. A fight about food would do nothing for their having a good time.

Max looked up at the clock. It was eight am. She needed ten minutes to walk to school, five to process through the doors, and then, fingers crossed, she could make it to first period without being a target for the bullies.

She pushed her chair back, stretched her arms, and had started to leave the room when her mom cleared her throat.

Max turned to look at her. "What?"

"I thought we were going to start working on our domestication skills? I would hate for my genius daughter to fail homemaking," her mother said.

Max didn't know what to think of her mom. She always had this sardonic tone. It confused the hell out of Maxine. *Does she want me to care or not?* Max sighed. She grabbed the plate and scraped the contents into the composter. *This is going to be some interesting birthday*, she thought.

The walk from Max's house to the high school was just long enough that her backpack started to rub the fronts of her shoulders. Her arms tingled, and beads of sweat trickled down her face like it always did, even on crisp autumn mornings like today. She prayed the powder wouldn't wear off.

The two-story, all-red-brick high school loomed ahead. It appeared warm and inviting, but Max never felt invited there. The line of teenagers going into the building moved fast today.

If she entered the school too quickly, the homeroom's doors would still be locked, which meant she'd have to roam the hallways. The corridors held crevices and corners that were not picked up by the cameras. Max could easily be pushed into a space where she would be poked with a pencil, slammed against a wall, or have her homework ripped apart.

The wand beeped in rhythm as each teen's ankle bracelet was swept.

According to the weekly community meetings, the ankle bracelets were meant to keep the teens safe. Maxine had heard that before the war, teenagers had been free to do as they pleased, wear what they wanted, say whatever was on their mind, but so many of them had died that the community had agreed they must now be tracked and controlled.

The tracking device was annoying, but Max was used to it. It was inevitable. She'd received it on her thirteenth birthday, just like everyone else. The seniors had been wearing them for at least four to five years. Who was Max to say anything about what was right or wrong about the government?

Mr. Dakotas smiled at Max as she walked up to the entrance, awaiting the scan of her bracelet. "Good morning, Maxine. Are you ready for that quiz?" He quickly swept the wand across her ankle.

He looked at the reading, then looked up at Max. "I know you'll do fine," he said as he waved Max through to the body scanner.

A large metal scanner loomed in the entry as an archway into a different dimension. Inside this place, rival rulers waged war, with the little people like Max as casualties to be pillaged. Max looked down the hallway toward her locker. She gulped.

As if on queue, the glowing girls huddled by the water fountain. Max's locker was two down from there. She remembered she had put on deodorant this morning. Her clothes were clean. She had brushed her teeth. Her hair was in place. Her feet dragged as she mentally checked off everything they had ever picked on her over.

The hems of their skirts swayed back and forth across their knees as they whispered amongst themselves. They all wore their hair in ponytails, with matching scarves. Max hated the scarves; they were just one more thing that contrasted her pale white skin.

She kept her head down, dialing her locker combination. She opened the door and started stuffing her books into the back, trying to move as stealthily as her pudgy arms would let her. She looked in the mirror on her locker door for one second, making sure the powder had not smeared onto her top.

Her moment of vanity cost her.

The locker door came forward so fast that it narrowly missed smacking her in the face. The noise turned the four girls' attention toward her. They scowled at the interruption of their conversation, until they saw that Nathan Nevada was the one who had slammed the locker.

Then they laughed.

Max had dropped her bag, spilling the contents onto the floor. She bent down to pick up the papers. Nathan stepped on her Trigonometry homework. She gritted her teeth in frustration. Nathan knew Mr. York took off points for poor presentation, regardless of whether or not all the answers were correct.

"Ah, that stinks, Max-een. Looks like you won't be the top-ranked student of the day." He smiled devilishly. "Humility is good for a person's character."

"What a narcissistic jerk," Maxine grumbled as Nathan casually strolled away.

Maxine thought something seemed weird about him today, but she couldn't quite figure it out. His blonde hair was swept over to the side like normal. He was wearing a crisp white T-shirt under a cornflower-blue button-up shirt. Max was sure it was his favorite, because he wore it enough. His khaki pants were pressed, but just rumpled enough that he looked casually cool instead of a like a slob. She could tell it was his way of rebelling, but today was different.

She hated herself for knowing all the details of a guy who made an art of making her miserable.

Her thoughts were interrupted as she watched perfectly-shaped legs march across her schoolwork in shiny black loafers, one by one. Today, she would go down to third or fourth in the rankings. It was the one thing she had that they couldn't compare to: she regularly topped them all academically.

But they all looked healthy, and she looked like

a round pale pile of childlike dough, while they all blossomed into adults. She crumpled the papers as she scooped them up and shoved them back into her bag. At this point, her grades were ruined for the day anyway. If she would be reprimanded, might as well make it count.

Max looked up at the hall clock. Five minutes to the bell, and there was not a moment to spare. Her heart raced. Homeroom would be nearly full. There'd be no seats left except at the front of the room—a place that Max dreaded.

In the front, you were the center of attention, the paper-pusher, and when you stood for roll call, everyone's eyes stared through you. She didn't want any more negative attention than usual.

By Max's calculations, there would be four front seats empty. She would have to sit in one, and be solely responsible for all the duties. The laughs and snickers of her classmates still echoed in her ears from the last time she'd gotten stuck with the job.

The door was still open, which meant Ms. Maine had not started roll call, announcements, or the daily pledges. Max sighed with relief. She slid into the second seat of the first row, trying to play it cool.

Her relief was short-lived. If she was in the front row, then who was missing? She was dying to know who had dared not come to school. As Ms. Maine talked about how each student should show initiative as a leader at McCarthy High, and she really wished that volunteers would step up, it occurred to Max that there were only four glowing girls today.

There should have been five. Ellen Pennsylvania was missing.

Missing school was a huge deal. A nurse came to your house to validate the illness, and then you were expected to come to school on Saturday after community meeting to repay the time. A glowing girl would never spend her Saturday afternoon in school if she could avoid it.

Ellen's father was medical director of the Rothgen Medical Institute. Would he *let* his daughter get sick? No one ever talked about being ill. People were expected to maintain their health so they could contribute to the betterment of McCarthy and Rothgen.

Max shifted in her seat. It made her nervous, thinking about getting sick. Her teachers were eyed her, and though they encouraged her scholastic achievement, many showed disdain for her body. She knew it was because she didn't look like everyone else.

Ms. Maine kept talking, but Max didn't hear her. She handed the notifications behind her mindlessly.

Ellen Penn, as the glowing girls called her, should have been at school.

The bell clanged for first period. At least Max could get the worst class of the day out of the way: gym.

CHAPTER 2

"That freckled redhead's heart rate is up a little higher than normal," a thin, balding man said as he recorded the reading. He gently maneuvered the remote control for the cameras that allowed him to scan the gymnasium.

"What about our little fatty?" an old man with paper-thin skin asked.

"That one is going to be a dud," the other man huffed as he looked at heart rate monitors and infrared heat patterns.

"I knew her mother," the old man said as he twisted his cane. "I think you might be wrong about that."

"Have you actually *seen* her? The girl barely moves. She isn't going to be one of them," he said, pointing at the screen.

And at that exact moment, the little fatty showed them something new.

RUDE AWAKENINGS

The gymnasium was massive. The glossy wooden floors felt like they went on forever, and the ceiling made Max dizzy. She was staring up at it when the leather volleyball smacked her cheek so hard that ringing screamed through her ears and pain seared her face. As the ringing decreased, a crescendo of laughter took over. The laughs echoed around the gym, and she felt the ball go thump, thump, thump by her feet.

"Hey Mess-a-shits-ett, pay attention or next time you might get knocked out."

Sue wasn't a glowing girl, but she was tall and

25

sturdy. Playing sports in gym class allowed her to excel in a place where in other classes she failed.

Normally her aggressive behavior was ignorable. As Max picked up the volleyball to toss it to the server, her throat tightened. The small hairs on the back of her neck stood up, and her normally slow pulse sped up until it felt like her heart would explode.

"Are you going to throw the ball or what?" Sue yelled.

The blood pulsed through Max's body so hard that she was sure every vein that crawled up her neck and face was ready to pop. Her fingernails dug into the volleyball. Before Max could rationalize the feelings, her body reacted. The ball hit Sue square in the nose.

Without thinking Max's mouth flew open: "I hate your stupid flipping face!" The scream was magnified by the shock of silence.

Mouths were agape as wide eyes looked back and forth between Max and Sue. Blood seeped through Sue's fingers as she tried to put pressure on her nose. Max felt like she was seeing Sue through a telescope while the other part felt like she was sitting in the bleachers watching someone else act in her place.

As her heart started to slow, her legs wobbled, and she slid to her knees. Slow deep breaths replaced her rapid, ragged breathing. She felt completely in her body again.

The gym teacher ran to Sue with a towel. No one came to check on Max. Everyone circled Sue as though they were protecting her from Max.

A crooked smile spread across her face. The littlest student in the entire school put fear in the heart of all the healthy young women, she thought. Her elbows pressed into her knees as she kept her head propped up with her hands.

On the gym floor, a shadow crossed over Max. She turned her head to see Nathan walking across the bleachers. His face grim as he jumped down, then exited through the door to the school hallway. *An odd look for an odd day*, Max thought.

The principal, Mr. Oregon, opened the door and pointed to Max. He proceeded to curl his finger back and forth, beckoning for Max. Her smile evaporated because Max had only encountered the principal when he was giving her awards for academic achievement.

There was no arguing what had happened. The cameras never lied. They watched and recorded every word said, every move made. As Max came closer, she noticed he backed away. He stepped aside to let her through the door, and as she walked past him, she felt the cold, hard grip of his wrinkled hand through the collar of her shirt. He guided her as though he were carrying a bad little dog by the scruff of its neck.

Apparently, academic achievement does not trump breaking someone's nose, Max thought as the principal shoved her into a plastic chair outside his office, then slammed the door.

"She finally did it!" Mr. Oregon screamed. He lowered his voice after and the words became an angry muffle.

Max leaned her sweaty head against the wall, closed her eyes and thought, Happy fucking Birthday to me.

Max's mother gave her a blank look as she passed by her and into the principal's office. Max was surprised. She was sure her Mom would be pissed. Instead, there was a weird twinkle in her eyes that looked like fear trying to creep up.

There was no way her Mom and Dad would be punished; her actions had felt uncontrollable, but they'd still been hers. She strained to hear what the two adults were discussing. She was distracted by Ellen Penn's mother entering the front office.

Her deep, dark brown eyes were circled with sadness. She gave a weak smile to the secretary, who got up from the desk and walked around to hug her. Max tried to read their lips, but she was too far away. She thought she saw the words sorry and locker. The ladies walked out of the office and headed down the hall. Max strained her neck to see where they were going.

Curiosity gnawed at her. Where was Ellen and why was her Mom here? Maxine reeled with rules, regulations, and catastrophic conclusions when she felt something sharp poke her in the temple. She looked at her lap, a crumpled paper wad lay there as evidence of her injury. She looked up to see Nathan as he ran off.

Is it possible to have a crush on someone you want to kill? The creepy part of her that had an infatuation with Nathan wanted to keep the paper wad and hide it in the bottom of her sock drawer. Another part of her—the part that hated him and knew the way he treated her wasn't okay—wanted to set it on fire and shove it down his throat.

She'd already broken someone's nose; she thought better of attempting to asphyxiate someone else on the same day. She shoved the wad of paper into her backpack.

As Maxine's mother neared the door, she recognized the high pitched falsetto voice that meant her mother would rage later.

There was some serious anger brewing underneath her mom's skin that would erupt like a volcano when they got home. Maxine swallowed hard as the door opened. The smile on her mother's face was wide and forced, but under her masked pleasantry was something else. Max could feel it as goose bumps instinctually rose on her arm.

The principal looked at Max with a troubled expression. "Well, Max, your mother has agreed that your punishment for throwing the ball at Sue will be rank zero for the rest of the week, and you'll be in detention on Saturdays after community meeting for a month."

He stared through Max. The bitterness in his voice was obvious to her. He didn't believe the punishment was tough enough.

She looked down at the floor and mumbled, "Yes sir."

Her mother added, "You'll still do all your homework, and do it well. Let's go." Her mother charged out of the office. Max grabbed her bag and ran after her.

Her mother's posture began to relax a little as they neared home, but her lips were still pursed tightly. After another block of silence, Maxine's mother let her have it.

"You realize you're going to lose your rank because someone called you a mess, right? Seriously. Flipping? Where did you get that word? If you're going to get in trouble, you should at least curse correctly. Jesus, I know those girls bully the hell out of you, but I thought you were better than that." Her mother stopped and looked at Max. "What was different?"

It took Max a minute to think about what had happened that was different today. She had been smacked in the face, kicked in the butt, tripped in the hallway, and never once had she retaliated.

She knew what had happened.

Her body had taken over and an adrenaline surge from hell had kicked in. It didn't seem normal. The experience was so extreme she couldn't explain how she'd had the strength to throw the ball so hard and fast.

She didn't have a response she wanted to share with her Mom, so she went with the easiest: "I dunno."

Her mother threw her arms up. "Wow, a 4.5 grade point average, years of spending hours after school helping you excel, and the only thing you can say is, 'I dunno.' That's just awesome. Your intelligence is all you have. You know that, right?"

The rest of the walk home was in silence. Max

wanted to share with her Mom what had happened, but it scared her so much, she didn't have the courage. Her Mom would figure it was hormones and let it go.

Maxine's mother had been a nurse before the war. In Maxine's opinion, her mother was one of the toughest women she knew, why would she expect Max to take being bullied forever? It was time for Maxine to start saying no to all the people who thought it was okay to shove her around.

Ellen Penn still stuck out in her mind. Max thought about the glowing girl from her homeroom class, her blonde hair so white and silky Max was sure it would look like shards of crystal under a microscope.

Her skin was so smooth and pink, her body perfectly-shaped... it made Max sick with envy, how pretty she looked. Maxine would never look like that in a million years. When Maxine looked at Ellen, she was also confused by the weird feelings inside of her. Ellen was so beautiful, it made her want to touch the girl in ways she didn't even understand.

MAXINE

Six houses from their own, her mother stopped. Max looked at her mom. Erin's lip trembled and her eyes filled with tears.

"What's wrong?" Max tugged on her mother's hand, trying to snap her out of whatever was freaking her out.

"When we get to the house, look down at the ground, walk straight into the house, go to your room. Do not say a word. Do you understand me?" Erin's voice shook.

"Yes, ma'am." Max looked ahead.

One of McCarthy's Suits leaned against his silver regulation car as he talked to her dad. The man appeared relaxed. Max's father shifted his weight back and forth. The McCarthy Suits—or M.S.—were enforcers of the community laws. They drove around patrolling the town for even the slightest of infractions, but they didn't usually go after kids, as far as she knew.

CHAPTER 3

"I'm on it," Justin Texas said into the mic.

He shook his head. Staying clean-shaven, parting his hair, and dressing like a gentleman annoyed him. But what was worse was the cognitive dissonance of old and new technology creating "the best of both worlds".

There wasn't anything *best* about McCarthy. It wasn't Houston. So as far as he was concerned, it was hell.

He looked down at the case file. Maxine Massachusetts didn't look like the type to pop off. She'd consistently been one of the sheeple, and as far as he was concerned, the hype about her was bullshit her floofy father had made up. Justin didn't think he even was the girl's real father.

And he *knew* that opinionated feminazi wasn't her mother. The woman had probably had her ovaries removed so she couldn't possibly populate the earth with more men. She'd run her mouth for about a year after getting here. At least the man had shut his mouth pretty quickly and gotten into the swing of things. That's a lawyer for you.

Justin got out of his car and started up the sidewalk to the house. He didn't have to go far, because Rob Massachusetts was out the door and headed towards him.

"M.S. Texas, how are you?" Rob asked. He took wide steps toward Justin, trying to put as much space between himself and the house.

"I'm doing okay. Yourself?" Justin said. In his training, they'd tried to beat out his accent, but it always seemed to slip.

"I'm good. What can I help you with?" Rob pushed his glasses up on his nose. He looked like he was trying not to tremble.

"Well, it seems we got a problem with little Maxine," Justin drawled out, remembering the old days, back when interrogation was actually difficult.

"We've got her under control," Rob said, crossing his arms. "She hasn't even developed like the rest of them. I told Rothgen what she could do."

"Look, I'm just here to let you know, we'll be keeping an eye on her. We don't want any more messes," Justin said.

Justin looked down the street. Erin Massachusetts was headed towards them with the little chubby homely thing.

Sometimes he wished Erin had been the one to go to law school; maybe then she'd know when to shut up.

SUITS, GLOWING GIRLS, AND INSPECTIONS

Maxine stared out her bedroom window and watched her parents talk to the M.S.

She could not see her parents' faces, but she could plainly see the face of the man who caused extreme hate and anger in her father. The top of his hair was a deep black—almost the color of Max's hair—but at his temples grey streaks ran back to his neckline.

He wore his dark navy suit with pride. It was crisp and clean even though it was mid-afternoon.

39

His arms were crossed over his chest and he smiled crookedly when he wasn't speaking. He wore sharp pointed boots with steel tips that were definitely not regulation.

The steel-grey car had a gloss to it that Max believed would be liquid like mercury if she touched it. It appeared monstrous and foreign on a normally-empty street.

Vehicles were meant for only those that held special positions in their society, someone like a major government agent—a suit, as they liked to call them, a person who didn't have to follow the rules of a community. The only rules they followed came from the City Upon the Hill, unlike regular adult members of the community, who needed to be able to walk at least ten miles.

Max dreaded her eighteenth birthday, when she would be required to walk with everyone else. Unless she figured a way to significantly change the way her body worked, she'd fail the test. She'd only seen the kids after they'd come back. Their faces were sunburned, they looked defeated with sagging shoulders and dirt covering their clothes.

The walk to school with a backpack was hard enough on her. She already came home with irritated thighs and sweat under her sweater from the effort of getting through the day.

She settled back into studying the conversation below. Why was a Suit in front of her house? Was she going to be arrested for hitting Sue in the face with a volleyball? Very few people were arrested in the community. It seemed that if people didn't fit in, they were transferred to another community where they might have a better chance.

They wouldn't transfer her parents. Maxine's father had an important job in government. He had been a lawyer before the war, and had helped make sure that all of the laws and regulations set forth by the big government were legal. He went to the Capitol to advocate on the part of their area all the time. They wouldn't make him leave.

The Suit looked up at Max's window, as though he knew she watched his every move. She stepped away and flopped onto the bed. She laid flat and stared at the white ceiling, which had a star pattern on it, repeated over and over in some weird goop.

On days when her mind felt like it would overwhelm her, she'd lie on the bed and count the number of edges that poked down from the star patterns.

The first person who came into her mind was Nathan. The blonde-haired, blue-eyed devil always seemed to fill every spare space in there.

Being crapped on was not cool. It didn't take a genius I.Q. to know that a girl should not like a boy who hurt her feelings and made fun of her, but something inside drew her to him.

There was an undertone to his words, a way he looked at her that signified comradery. A desire to be the best academically? Parents who expected perfection? She knew what made them kindred spirits was not that he felt bullied like her. Nathan had been one of the most loved kids in the class since she could remember.

The paper wad was still in her backpack. It would've been better if she'd tossed it, but... he'd thrown it at her.

Her justification for keeping it, if she were honest with herself, it was something he'd touched and now it belonged to her. She sat up and pulled the crumpled ball out, and ironed it as best she could. Her mouth dropped. Written in bold red letters, it read, "The time is coming when your world will change. Be ready or you will end up dead."

Her mother opened the door and peeked her head in. "Max, you can come downstairs now."

The voice startled Max. She fell off her bed, slipping the paper underneath before her mother could see it.

"Do you think you can keep from doing something destructive for about five minutes?" Her mother asked Max, in a much weaker sarcastic tone than normal.

Max nodded and smiled. There would be no reason to increase the amount of drama milling in their family tonight. She pushed herself up from the floor and followed her mother down the stairs to talk about what had happened at school.

The dinner table was quiet.

Max was accustomed to smiling faces and happy conversations from her parents. Now, instead, her father stared ahead, silently chewing his mashed potatoes like they were made of paper. Her mother looked through her father.

Max watched as her mother traced the floral wallpaper pattern back, forth, up, and down. Her mother's nerves must have been bad all day; the cherry wood dining room table shined as though it had several coats of wax on it.

Max couldn't eat now, either. She wanted to ask her Dad if he had heard anything at the Community Hall about someone petitioning for sick leave from school, or being homeschooled. However, this was not the night to bring up Ellen Pennsylvania.

Her father finally swallowed the mouthful of mashed potatoes, and took a swig of water from his amber-colored glass. Then he cleared his throat before speaking.

"Max, I'm disappointed in you. I'm an important member of this community and you could have caused me to lose my job today. If my own daughter can't follow the rules of non-violence, how can anyone take me seriously?" He didn't look at Max. He continued to stare through

Erin, while Erin continued to trace the pattern of the wallpaper.

The words didn't really match her father's expression at all. He continued, "You'll take your punishment gladly, give up your commissary vouchers to Sue York, and do whatever is asked of you in detention. Do you understand me?"

He never looked at her.

Max looked down at her plate. "Yes, sir."

"I'm glad that's cleared up. Every member of this society must be fit and healthy at all times. You could jeopardize Sue's future. It is required of you to assimilate. You weren't even thinking about that, I'm sure, when you were flinging volleyballs in people's faces. Go to your room. We can have cake tomorrow, and I'm not sure if you're going to get any of the gifts from me and your Mom."

His face never changed expression. It felt like he was reading from a script, and he wasn't a good actor.

"Okay, Dad." She pushed herself away from the table and went over to kiss her father on the cheek. Then she looked to her mother, who now appeared to be somewhat alert again, but her eyes were tired and glossy. She threw a kiss to her mother and walked out of the dining room and up the stairwell.

She wanted to cry, but she was so distracted by the missing Ellen and her own weird, out-of-body experience. What would happen if Ellen Penn didn't show up again tomorrow? Would anyone say anything?

Part of her felt anger at her father. He knew she would never fit in this community, and unless there was a miracle, she would never be fit and healthy like the other students. Now there was also this other problem she had to make sure never happened again.

Maybe Nathan's note was prophetic, and her life was changing. She might not end up physiologically dead, but she might just *wish* she was.

Max's favorite place to spend her fifteen-minute break after lunch was the girls' bathroom at the end of the yellow hall next to the stairwell. It was the smallest bathroom, with the worst lighting, and the other girls rarely used it.

It was the perfect hiding place for a girl trying to stay out of the way of bullies. Max loved to sit on the radiator situated in the furthest stall from the door, even when it was in the middle of winter and it felt like it might burn through her skirt, blistering her skin. She was always so cold that it felt amazing.

In the spring, when they shut it off, she felt like her bones would freeze and shatter with the wrong move. However, she still came in here, sitting on the radiator and looking out the window at the athletic fields. Nathan played every sport, so he was always out there, either training or goofing around with the other guys from the various teams he played on.

Her mom had told her that before the war, people had traveled from all kinds of cities to play each other at sports. The kids had sat in the stands and screamed for their home team. Now, the kids only played against one another in what they called intramural teams.

In the past there were cities so big that they

might have six high schools just in one town. The idea of a place so huge scared Max a little. There were about a hundred families living in her community—if families were what you wanted to call them.

Each group of people was asked to identify what state it was from upon entrance into the community. The government then put them into families, accordingly.

Max's father was from Massachusetts, and her mother never talked about where she'd come from. She said she'd met Maxine's father on the road, trying to survive together, and they'd agreed that through it all they would live and die together.

Max rolled her eyes at her mother's dramatic remarks about her undying pledge to stand by her Dad.

She sipped from her canteen of lukewarm tea as she watched out the window for any signs of Nathan playing football or running with the other guys. Just as she saw him saunter onto the field, the door to the bathroom creaked open.

She quickly screwed the lid onto her canteen

and pulled her feet up on the radiator. She couldn't afford for anyone to know she'd found a safe haven from torture, even if it was for such a short amount of time.

"Do you think anyone is in here?" a familiar female voice asked.

It sounded like Karlene Indiana. She was nice like Ellen, but when pushed acted as bad as the rest of them.

"Who would want to even pee in this creepy restroom? This place is gross," Nancy Oregon said, her voice filled with revulsion.

If Nancy and Karlene were in here, the other two remaining glowing girls couldn't be far behind. The slapping of loafers on the tiled floor indicated that Marie Washington and Esther Hampshire were not far behind.

"Hey, we need to talk. There hasn't been a safe place for us to talk since Ellen was taken away," Esther said.

Esther Hampshire was known by most as Evil Esther for her hateful ways and ability to find weakness in people and gut them with it, but now her voice sounded soft and scared. She'd said that Ellen had been taken away. Where would Ellen have been taken?

"We're not supposed to talk about this," Marie whined.

"Look, Nancy overheard her dad on the phone with Ellen's dad. Something serious was wrong with her. They aren't going to talk about it. They're taking her off the school roster as though she never existed. How can they do that? They only make bad people disappear. Ellen wasn't bad. She was obedient, fit, and at an appropriate level of intelligence to keep her place. If they were going to pull some unworthy student out, it wouldn't have been her," Esther rationalized with the other girls.

"What if she was sick and her father was hiding it?" Karlene asked.

"She wasn't sick. Her father is the medical director of the training facility. He would know if his own child were ill. Did they say anything about her being dead?" Esther asked. Max wanted to peek through the slots of the stall and watch them banter back and forth, but she was afraid that they would see her, and then her secret spot would be ruined.

Nancy spoke softly. "No. They didn't come out and say that she was dead. They just said she would be removed from the rosters and that all the teachers were to be notified. All the other adults would be notified at the weekly meeting."

The restroom door swung open swiftly, hitting the wall behind it. "Girls, are you planning to go to class or hang out here all afternoon?" Ms. Maine demanded. "The bell is about to ring."

Max gulped. She would be late if all of these people did not get out of here so she could exit privately.

Esther spoke up. "We were just discussing what to wear to community meeting on Saturday."

"I know it is a huge event socially, but your academics are the most important thing when you are here," Ms. Maine said dryly.

All four of the girls giggled nervously as they shuffled out of the restroom. As the door began to close, Max put her feet down on the floor. She'd started slide the latch of the stall door when she noticed Ms. Maine was standing in front of the mirror.

Her face normally looked so young and smooth, but today, she had wrinkles in the corners of her eyes. Ms. Maine looked in the mirror and blotted tears from her face. She mumbled softly to herself: "What happened? How did we get here? Why? Why? How did they get all the control? *How*?"

Ms. Maine cried for several minutes before the bell rang, shaking her back to reality.

This fifteen-minute break felt like the longest time in Max's short life. What did all of the adults know that they were holding back from the kids? None of the kids remembered the war or what had come before it. They only knew what the community wanted them to know.

Could they really just pull an innocent girl from her life and make her disappear? Ellen Penn was one of the healthiest kids Max had ever met. She never ranked as high as Max, but she could hold her own with many of the other students.

Max wasn't sure if she was more scared of the fact the glowing girls knowing something she had not picked up on or her homeroom teacher looking like she was going to lose her mind at any moment.

Max wanted to think about this more, but she was going to be late to class. After Ms. Maine left, Max stepped out into the hall, looking both ways before heading to chemistry. Out of the corner of her eye, she saw Mr. Oregon, the principal, leaning on the wall at the intersection where yellow hall met blue.

She gulped. As much as she wanted to keep her hiding spot, she had a suspicion it was gone forever now. The glowing girls had brought attention to themselves, and now Max as well, by breaking their routine.

History class was such a bore for Maxine. They had repeated the same history every year since she had started school. Facts, dates, and events had been memorized years before and stuck with Max without hesitation when asked to be recalled.

They not only had to take the class, but also, at the beginning of community meeting, all the children went to classrooms and watched a video each week.

Max thought about the incident in the restroom.

She had never thought of the glowing girls as people who thought about anything except looking great and making others feel miserable. It was a weird feeling, to empathize with their fear of losing Ellen Penn. Even if Max sometimes wished all of the glowing girls would disappear off the planet, it still scared the hell out of her to imagine someone just disappearing while the adults erased the evidence.

She sat and started outlining all of the things that had happened since she'd woken up on her birthday.

She wasn't worried about the lecture; she could sit here and spout out history while continuing to write. Besides, she was going to receive a zero for all material this week anyway. What did she have to lose?

"Maxine Massachusetts, can you tell us the day the old world started to end?" Mr. Idaho asked sharply.

Max sighed. She had been targeted before she really had a chance to start. Mr. Idaho was going to try to make an example out of her for not paying attention. "Which date do you mean, sir?"

She looked up to see Mr. Idaho leaning on his wooden desk at the front of the classroom. He grabbed his chin, rubbing it before he spoke again. "Well, I asked you if you could tell us the day the world started to end. Do you know the answer?" One of her classmates snickered over in the corner.

"Sir, there are many days the world started to end. Which country would you like? Do you want the theorized version of where the virus started? Do you want the day people started biting and eating other people, or the day the governments collapsed? I still need to know what country you want. The world used to be a big place, from what I understand…"

Suddenly, the excitement of one-upping the teacher exhilarated Max. She felt the rush of blood zoom through her veins as her heartbeat started to accelerate. She clenched her teeth as the wild feeling that had caused her to throw the ball at Sue York's face rushed over her again. Her pencil snapped in half under the pressure of her thumb.

"Whoa, little girl, those are some seriously

complex questions for someone your age to be asking," Nathan Nevada said loudly. The class laughed. Nathan looked at Mr. Idaho and said, "I think the date you are inquiring about is June 14, 1998. It's the day that the former United States government realized that a bioterrorism weapon was unleashed on all major countries in the world. The United States declared Martial Law and requested the help of—at the time—the private contractor Rothgen."

"Good job, Nathan. Glad to see that someone still listens in class without questioning authority." Mr. Idaho walked around his desk, looking at Maxine as he wrote in his grade book.

The rest of the class was silent. It seemed like all the students were sitting up straighter except for Maxine. She was slumped over, still calming down from the rush of her temporary rebellion.

She looked at Nathan. He sat at his desk, cool as ever, leaning slightly back in the chair, his eyes focused on the front of the classroom. Max tried to telepathically send him a message to stay the hell out of her way, but he appeared as oblivious to her existence as ever.

The bell rang for the end of the day. She had just been marked down as being disobedient. The week was getting better and better.

CHAPTER 4

"Sorry to hear about Ellen, Doc," the med tech said as she stood at the counter and organized stacks of papers, placing them on clipboards.

"It happens." Dr. Pennsylvania shrugged.

"But she was your bio-kid. You didn't adopt her." The med tech stopped. "It's different."

"You think so?" the doctor asked. He grabbed the clipboard and tapped at a line graph. "Make sure you are recording those hormone levels each week and comparing them to the daily thermal scans from the school."

The med tech looked down at the papers,

pretending to be interested. "Yes, sir."

Dr. Pennsylvania handed the clipboard back to her. "They aren't our children. They're Rothgen's. *You're* Rothgen's. It would do you good to remember that."

He walked over to the window and looked out to see the children lining up for inspection. He felt a quiver in his gut; he guessed it was the closest he'd feel to an emotion about Ellen.

Rothgen recruited the best and brightest of those who couldn't feel empathy for others. As much as he tried, he ultimately knew he needed to save his own ass at all costs. Ellen's problem wasn't going to keep him alive.

THE INSPECTION

Max rolled over in bed and watched the hour hand tick to seven on her small, round, silver alarm clock. It was Saturday morning. She pulled her pillow over her face, thanking no one in particular that the rest of week had gone by without incident.

The urge to strike out had disappeared, but anxiety over the disappearance of Ellen Penn had taken its place.

Ms. Maine had carried out the homeroom routine each morning, passing out papers, and saying pledges. She did her regular speeches about leadership and being a good citizen of the community, as calm and pleasant as ever.

Max had scanned the room, looking for signs that others were concerned that Ellen Penn was gone. If they were, they didn't show it. Maybe their parents had already talked to them. The glowing girls' parents had talked to *them* about being quiet.

Which brought Max to a whole other issue: why had *her* parents not mentioned that Ellen was gone? Her Dad worked in the main government offices; people in the community respected him. If a law was broken, it was her father's job to mediate.

Wouldn't Ellen's Dad go talk to him, if the Suits had come into their house and grabbed her? At this point, Max didn't know who to trust, but she couldn't imagine her mother or father tolerating her being pulled away from them.

She wanted to smother herself into unconsciousness, but she couldn't afford to miss community meeting and physical inspections. Her feet felt like lead as she swung them over the side of the mattress. She ceremoniously made her bed, tucking in the corners tight, then smoothed out the wrinkles, eliminating any flaws.

Max imagined some invisible troll came into your room searching for imperfections, ready to rip you apart like some bad faery tale. The reality was that families lost commissary vouchers over failed inspections. A good kid would never want their family to starve because their room was messy. As far as Max knew this had never happened. It was all a ruse to get kids to clean.

Max pressed the bristle brush against her scalp and stroked downward. No matter how many times she brushed, little waves of misshapen curls poked out.

She looked at her clothes again. She decided on a white button-up shirt, brown cardigan, and pleated pink skirt to try to fit into today. Plus, detention afterward would be less difficult if she appeared to fit in.

Her loafers were polished, her socks were straight up to her knees, and each pleat of the skirt was pressed. Her ankle bracelet stuck out, as usual.

"Are you ready?" Max's mother asked, opening the door.

Max nodded. She looked down at her hands.

MAXINE

She didn't want her Mom to see that she was scared to attend meeting today.

"I know you hate inspections, but there are reasons for all of this. When we walked through the gates to live here, we all signed a pact. We agreed..." Her mother's voiced trailed off. Max saw her staring sadly out the window as she squeezed Max's shoulders. Max shook her off. It brought her Mom back to life.

"If your father and I can live with it after understanding the world before, you'll be okay." She rubbed Max's shoulders again, and smoothed down her dull, wiry black hair.

"I know, Mom," she mumbled as she stood to follow her out of the room.

Max's father held the front door open so the women could walk through. Max noticed that his shirt was significantly stiffer than usual, and she smelt the burnt starch as she passed him. He closed the door, but didn't lock it, per regulation for inspection day. Her father had told her a long time ago that locks were useless. The Suits had the keys to everything.

The family walked up to the single-story community building. A small bell tower straddled the middle of the roof. Max mindlessly veered to the right and lined up behind the other children under age eighteen. Her parents entered the tall white double doors of the entrance.

Max felt a nudge on the back of her heel. She turned around to see Nathan Nevada smirking at her. "You look nice in pink, Maxine."

She turned around quickly so that he couldn't see her blush. Her heart raced at the thought of Nathan staring at her legs. Just at the moment she felt like she might pass out, her name was called to the booth.

There was a new inspector this week. Max recognized him. He was the boy who'd used to pick up the recycling. He looked determined to find a flaw.

She noticed he stared at the back of her heel for a long time. Nathan must have scuffed her shoe. She silently cursed his existence; the jerk was determined to kill her via heartbreak or have her thrown out of the community.

She held her breath in anticipation of a lecture. Instead, the young inspector scribbled something on his clipboard. He looked up and gave Max a tight-lipped smile. "You passed hygiene, Ms. Massachusetts. Time for health inspection."

After the inspector left, Maxine walked over to the hook on the back of the door and grabbed an examination gown off the hook. She removed her clothes and slipped the thin green cotton gown on. Then she sat down on the examination table and shivered as she waited for the med tech to enter. The room felt frigid today.

"Hey, Maxine, how's it going?"

Max felt a rush of relief at the sight of Gretchen, her favorite med tech. Max looked at the young woman's perfect olive skin. It glowed with radiance, and her hair was an amazing shade of brown, with tiny caramel highlights that seemed to twinkle in the light.

Gretchen's uniform accentuated her tiny waist and round hips. Max frowned. She bet the girl planned to marry a doctor, so she could move between communities if she wanted. She proceeded to take Max's temperature and blood pressure, and check her pulse.

The med tech read her mind. "I know, I know, you're wondering why I'm still here. Most girls only make it two to three years out of high school before they get married. I'm waiting for the perfect guy. The worst thing that could happen is that I stay single and work as a med tech longer. If it wasn't for single women with high expectations, there would be no women working in the communities."

Gretchen laughed. In Max's opinion, it was little too loud. She wrapped a tourniquet around Max's upper arm, then effortlessly pressed a needle into the crevice of her inner arm, drawing enough blood to fill several vials. The tourniquet snapped off, and she delicately pulled out the needle, placing it into a bin for disposal.

"It was good seeing you, Max. Dr. Penn will be in shortly. I'll be back to chaperone." She patted Max on the knee. She was already out the door when Max noticed that she'd left her chart.

Max saw her vital signs. Gretchen had circled

her heart rate and blood pressure. The rates were on a chart from every week's exams. The weird thing was that her rates had stayed the same until this week. Her heart rate was up twenty beats per minute, and her temperature was six degrees higher than normal.

She heard the door begin to open. Max jumped back onto the examination table as the Gretchen came back into the room.

"I forgot this! How silly of me." She grabbed the chart and walked out without making eye contact with Max.

I really am changing, thought Max.

Max kicked her legs back and forth, trying to stay warm as she waited for Dr. Pennsylvania. She wondered if his eyes would be sad, like his wife's. Should she ask him about Ellen? Would he tell her what had happened to her? It seemed like an hour before the doctor entered with Gretchen shortly behind him. He was tall and thin, with piercing blue eyes. He smiled blandly at Max.

"Hello Maxine. How have you been this week? I saw that you had a birthday a few days ago...

How'd that go for you?" The tone of Dr. Pennsylvania's voice sounded kind, but underneath Max felt an edge, as though he were searching for something.

"It was okay. No problems," Max said, smiling up at the doctor.

"No problems? Hmmmm. I hear you're going to detention after community meeting today. Do you consider that a problem?" Dr. Penn scribbled in the chart.

Max stayed silent. The doctor leaned in, placing the cold stethoscope on her chest. She could hear her own heartbeat, so loud she didn't think he really needed the tool. He leaned over, listening to her lungs through her back. She shivered from the cool touch of the metal rim.

He pushed Max back onto the table and began pressing on her abdomen. She didn't hurt anywhere, but it made her feel uncomfortable, the way he kept pushing at her liver.

"That doesn't hurt?" he asked.

"No," Max replied. She swallowed the nervous spit accumulating in her mouth before she gained the courage to ask, "How is Ellen doing, Dr. Penn? She hasn't been to school all week."

The doctor pulled Max to the sitting position and used a small mallet to hit her right knee.

Dr. Pennsylvania continued to watch her reflexes as he tapped each knee. "I'm sorry, what are you asking me?"

"Your daughter, Ellen. We've missed her at school, and they removed her from the roster. I just wanted to know..." Before Max could finish her sentence, Gretchen knocked over the small metal procedure tray behind the doctor. She glared at Max.

Dr. Penn turned around to the med tech and said sharply, "And that is *exactly* why women are no longer doctors." He waved his hand up in the air, dismissing the med tech to clean up the contents of the tray.

He then turned back to Max. "I don't know what you are babbling on about, but you appear to be physically fine. Put your clothes on and get to community meeting. If you're getting detention, you need to listen to the meeting more than anyone."

The doctor stood up, straightened his lab coat, and walked past the crouched Gretchen, who was tossing gauze in the trash. Her lips were pursed together as she looked at the ground. When she finished picking up the tray, she backed out of the room, her eyes still glued to floor.

Maxine pulled on her shirt and skirt. She readied herself for the public humiliation.

CHAPTER 5

"She isn't going to buy this. I've never talked to her, I haven't even been within fifty feet of her." The pale young man rubbed his hands through his short black hair. The blue veins on the side of his face throbbed. He pushed himself further back in the hard wooden chair and crossed his arms. He'd been following orders for as long as he could remember

"Do what you're told. We've kept you from her for a reason. Do you understand me? You're older, a student teacher. That's enough," Dr. Pennsylvania said.

The young man looked from his father, to the

73

principal, to the girl's father. All three surrounded the principal's desk.

"Yes sir," he mumbled.

"Just be careful. She's shy, but opinionated," her father instructed. "I don't know if she is going to be able to handle the attraction. She might run."

Dr. Pennsylvania laughed. "Oh, she won't run. He might be the one running, after the virus kicks in. These girls go crazy like dogs in heat."

"I don't really care for you comparing my daughter to a menstruating dog."

"These aren't our kids anymore. Maxine is just one of many," Dr. Pennsylvania countered.

"Dad, she's still a person. I'm a person too, you know," Ray quipped.

"You stopped being a person a long time ago. You're lucky we keep you alive. You killed your sis—" Dr. Pennsylvania's face turned crimson and his nostrils flared.

"Enough!" Mr. Oregon said, slamming his hand on the desk. "Let's get this over with. Give Rothgen what they want. Our safety is the priority."

BOYS

"On June 14, 1998, the world heard the last president of the United States declare Martial Law and allow our savior Rothgen Corporation to take command. The war raged for ten long years, but in the end, humanity survived one of the most horrendous epidemics the world has ever seen. Now, the communities developed and protected by Rothgen give humanity a chance to grow and thrive in ways that were never seen before the war. Individuals are equal, and food, healthcare, and shelter are available for everyone. Corben Rothman is our leader and savior…"

The video droned on for what seemed like hours. Max wanted it to be over. She wanted everything to be over. They would announce her name on the detention list, her offense, and she would have to stand in front of the crowd. Never in a million years had she expected to be one of those kids.

The video ended, and the lights brightened the room. Ms. Maine, who led the Rothgen Respect group on Saturday mornings, asked, "Well, does anyone have any questions before we head into the auditorium to join the adults?"

The large classroom was silent, except for the rustling of antsy teenagers ready to start their weekend.

"Okay then, head out to meeting and listen to announcements. You're excused." Ms. Maine waived the group toward the exit.

The teens with plans rushed excitedly towards the auditorium. Max noticed that everyone like her—those spending the afternoon in detention—slowly dragged themselves out the door.

Ms. Maine looked at Max. "It won't be too bad.

You'll get used to it. It's only a month. At least you're not on a twelve-week stint, like some of the other kids."

Max headed to the front to sit with her parents. She slid onto the polished wooden bench next to her mother. Max's mother wrapped her arm around her shoulders and squeezed tightly. Max knew that it would be an embarrassment for her parents when she was called up to be announced as an offender.

Mr. Oregon started his segment of community meeting by talking about inspections. They were at ninety-nine percent on hygiene compliance, and health was at ninety-six percent. He frowned after stating the health statistic.

"Parents," he said, "make sure your children are complying with bedtime regulations. Sleep deprivation can cause serious health concerns in the future and poor grades." He rustled through the crisp white papers before coming to the detention list. "The following students will be serving detention this week for the following infractions."

The principal went through several names, and Max watched as each student headed to the front and stepped on the stage. They called her name, but couldn't move her legs to stand up. Her mother nudged her slightly, and finally, Max stood.

As she went, her crime was announced as "retaliation." She had thought it would surely be "aggression." She walked forward, trying to keep her head high. Mr. Oregon never spoke of what she'd retaliated against, but it made her sound better than the volleyball-wielding psycho he had portrayed to her mother.

Several other names were recited, then the final name on the list was called. If Max had not seen her rise from her bench in the middle of the room, she wouldn't have believed it.

The principal called Sue York's name.

She walked up the stage stairs, and as her right foot hit the first step, her charge was called out: "provocation." Max tried to stare forward and not smile. Sue York was being punished for starting the incident.

For once, Max was glad there were cameras in the gym. Sue must have thrown the ball at her face on purpose. The black circles around her eyes made her look like a cartoon character as the white strips on her nose tried to hold it in place. Sue looked down at the floor, repentant for her crime.

"The children will serve their sentence per the guidelines of the school and community. They'll have these events on their records so long as they live here," Mr. Oregon said. He cleared his throat. "We do not take disobedience or roguish behavior lightly. Your parents have given us permission to mold you to become the citizens Rothgen needs for the world survive. Please also remember all children must meet the minimum requirements for health. Thank you."

Ms. Maine beckoned the motley crew of detainees on the stage toward her and the children trudged slowly off the stage, their feet dragging with each step.

Max looked at her Mom, but she stared intently into one of the corners of the auditorium. She looked a thousand miles away from the community meeting. Max wondered what was going through her mind. Was she upset to see her daughter going to detention? Did she wonder why Sue was also being punished?

Behind her, Max's father took to the podium to talk about ordinances and changes from the City Upon the Hill. His voice sounded pleasant but fake. It was the voice from the other night, when he'd talked to her about her punishment for throwing the ball at Sue York.

Max needed to focus on detention, not her parents. She wasn't sure what she would be doing in detention. Nonetheless, she filed in line with rest of the offenders as they walked down the street toward the high school. Max noticed the trees to her left were changing color. The flagrant reds, oranges, and browns of fall were accented by the mid-afternoon sun.

The group stopped for a moment before entering the school.

Out of the corner of her eye, Max spotted a silver car parked up the street. She squinted to see the driver; it was the Suit from outside her house. She turned back quickly, pretending to be focused on the head of a young woman who was chronically late.

KATIE CORD

The girl preferred to spend her Saturday afternoons in detention rather than be on time for class. Max's empathy level for such nonsense was significantly higher now that she had broken a rule herself. The group walked through the large double doors and into eerily silent halls.

Inside, the children were separated into two lines: those who had committed behavioral infractions like Max and Sue, and those who were sick, late, or academically weak students.

Max's group was directed toward one of the classrooms that held a film projector, while the other kids were led toward a standard one. The malingerers and chronically late walked slowly toward Ms. Maine.

Standing outside Max's room was Mr. Idaho, the history teacher. Maxine felt a lump in her throat. She was now being held captive by the person she'd recently annoyed the most. Instinctively, she looked at the marbled grey floor as she passed by him.

A hand grabbed her as she walked to back of the room. She turned and looked into eyes, black as night. They belonged to a stranger who was so pale she saw blue veins crawling from his temple towards his hairline.

He pulled her close to him and spoke in a low voice. "It's best you just sit up here so I don't have to lecture you about how I hate people who sit in the back."

Max nodded, and without thinking, flopped down in the nearest seat. She noticed he was wearing the traditional male teacher uniform: brown wool sport coat, tie, khakis, button-up shirt, but underneath she saw he wore a black t-shirt. He was getting away with violating regulations. Her stomach fluttered, and her face flushed red. She felt like she would vomit any minute.

"I'm Max," she said timidly.

"I know," the strange guy said, leaning over her desk and smiling devilishly. "Everyone knows you, Maxine. I'm Ray. But when we are in the classroom you can call me Mr. Penn."

His smile intoxicated her. It reminded her of a picture she'd seen in a book her mother had hidden. The character was a snake, smiling at a naked woman holding an apple. She felt like that woman, being tempted by something she shouldn't want. She smiled back at him softly, and then looked at her desk.

The door to the classroom shut, and Mr. Idaho walked across the room and sat down on his desk. He opened his attendance book.

As each name was called out, the student raised their hand. When Mr. Idaho reached Max's name, he looked up at her with a challenging twinkle in his eyes. She too raised her hand. She wasn't sure what he found so amusing.

Is Ray related to Ellen? Before Max's mind could think further on the subject, Mr. Idaho's voice interrupted her thoughts.

"Class, I want to first introduce you to Mr. Raymond Pennsylvania. He is a new student teacher here at McCarthy High. He is starting off observing detention so that he may understand the foundation on which our curriculum is based— something you folks seem to have forgotten.

"As you know, everyone in this class is being punished for an infraction that goes against school and community policy. It's my job as a history teacher and historian to remind all the students who have trouble living by our rules why we live the way we do and what could happen if we all tried to solve our problems the way that you chose to."

Mr. Idaho's voice filled with sincerity and conviction as he spoke to the assembled students. "I hope after your time in detention, you will understand how imperative it is for you to believe in the Rothgen Communities and what they stand for... So, with that, you'll be watching videos during your sentence. You're expected to stay awake, eyes on the screen at all times. Mr. Pennsylvania here will be taking notes and observing you."

"Mr. Greg Maryland, would you be so kind as to dim the lights?" Mr. Oregon asked. Greg Maryland complied, the room dimmed. Greg went from being the guy who cut up and laughed during class to the most obedient student in the school. He'd been in detention for as long as Maxine could remember. If she recalled correctly, he'd been the one who'd made a stink bomb in the chemistry lab.

He now sat with perfect posture in class with his hands clasped on top of his books. His hair was combed over with his shirt buttoned to the top.

Max looked at the front corner of the room to see what Ray was doing while she still had the chance. Her cheeks became hot as she realized he was looking at her. He smiled broadly at her this time, and rolled his eyes at Mr. Idaho as he walked toward the back of the room to start the projector.

She wanted to giggle, and Max was not a giggler. The light from the projector shined over their heads, casting a glow in the room. Ray pointed at his eyes using his index and middle fingers, then pointed at the screen. Max looked forward, and the smile faded from her face.

The person on the screen stared ahead, one eye socket hollow, the other filled with a milky pupil. The flesh on her face barely hung on. There were no more lips, just gnashing raw teeth, with receding gums. The hair had been long at one time, and looked to be blonde. The woman wore tattered clothes from the old world. Her skirt was above her mid-thigh—if it was a skirt. The shirt showed her shoulders and arms. Her breasts were strangely upright, compared to the sagging skin all around them.

Behind her, there were others like her: all rotting, wearing old-world clothes and milling around, looking lost and hungry.

"It's day forty-one here in Los Angeles. I know that I shouldn't be out filming, but all I've ever wanted to be is a filmmaker, and now I have the chance. Now that all the rest are dead. It was never my desire to be the best by default," a male narrator said in low voice.

The camera shook a little, and the young male narrator was silent. He sighed, then started again. "So, basically, there's a couple things that happen with these sick fucks. They start out as people, like you and me. They get sick. They look like they die. Then they come back to life, searching for a food source. Guess what the food source is, kid? It's you."

The camera focused on the shuffling people for a little while longer. Then the narrator decided to move. He mumbled under his breath as the camera faced the concrete. "Well, it's time to get the hell out of here. The bastards are still rotting and looking for flesh."

He started walking away, but off in the distance, Max could see movement. It was fiery red demon of a car, swerving back and forth as it went down the street. It was heading toward the driver. The view swerved as the narrator dunked down behind an overturned van. The image moved up and down as his breathing became more rapid.

The narrator whispered. "Assholes like these are more dangerous than the biters."

The urge to capture every moment left of the living must have overtaken the narrator's need to be safe as he peeked around the hood, attempting to film. The car had slowed down to a crawl.

There were two people inside the car, both appearing more ravenous and crazed than the dead. A gun poked out of the passenger window and shot at anything that moved. Loud music thumped. Their laughs could be heard over it when a walking dead fell to the ground.

MAXINE

The narrator watched in silence while the two got out of the vehicle and started walking around with their guns, shooting at anything that moved. They went into the stores that lined the street, taking items that looked like they might have been of value in their past life.

They were leaving a jewelry store when one of them looked across the street and spotted the narrator. He dropped his bounty and pointed his gun in the narrator's direction. He yelled, "Look over there, someone's spying on us!"

Their faces disturbed Max. For one thing, the passenger of the car had piercings in his face, but it wasn't just that that made him disturbing; it was that he looked as hungry to feed off of another human's misery as the dead girl had at the beginning.

Max looked over to see Ray staring at the screen. He wasn't impressed with the scenario. Max figured he must have seen this before, to have no feelings about what was happening on the screen.

She looked at his profile a little longer. She

watched as the sharp blue vein that ran down the side of his temple moved up and down occasionally.

His hair was so dark. She wanted to walk over and touch it…

"Ms. Massachusetts, eyes on the screen," Mr. Idaho said from the back of the room.

Ray looked over and smiled at her. He nodded at the screen. She turned to see the guy with the metal in his face fire his gun at the narrator. He fell sideways, the camera still facing his assailant. The guys laughed at what had happened.

Max felt cold all over. Sure, she had felt some kind of weird excitement and relief when she'd smashed in Sue York's face with the volleyball, but kill someone? Never.

"What would you do if you were alone and someone decided to hunt you down?" Mr. Idaho asked.

Silence. Maxine looked around the room. Everyone looked as lost as her.

George Dakota raised his hand.

"Yes?" Mr. Idaho addressed him.

"Well, uh, I'd run and hide until I could find a McCarthy Suit," George said. He sniffed nervously after talking. He reminded Maxine of a rabbit with his small nose and long front teeth.

Lucas Vermont, who sat to the right of Maxine, mumbled, "He doesn't know what is coming to him."

"Great answer, George." Mr. Idaho chuckled. He pointed to the door, "Let's head to the gym."

Maxine felt paralyzed. She wasn't expecting to go to gym. She watched as each student lined up as confused as she was. From what she understood, the worst penalty from detention was not having Saturday afternoon free.

"Ms. Massachusetts, did you think it was a suggestion? Move it," Mr. Idaho said, his voice full of sarcasm.

Maxine continued to sit, staring at the desk. She didn't have her gym clothes or shoes. How was she going to run around in her skirt and loafers?

"Ms. Massachusetts? We're going," Ray said. She looked up to see him pointing at the door. He smiled at her. She pushed herself up and followed

Ray.

In the gymnasium, the students stood in a row in front of Mr. Idaho. He paced back and forth as he sized each of them up.

"So, what would you do if there were no McCarthy Suits? No, Rothgen? No one to protect you?" His voice carried through the gym. "Get down on the floor and give me fifty push-ups. We're going to do what we used to call in the Navy a good old fashioned mash!"

Everyone dropped to their bellies and started pushing themselves up. Maxine tried as hard as she could to push upwards. Sweat beaded on her forehead, and her arms shook as she pushed up. It felt like forever.

Mr. Idaho stood over Maxine, "Maxine, if you don't do ten push-ups in the next five minutes then everyone else will do fifty more."

Maxine heard the groans. She pushed harder. Her breathing increased. She found the effort to push through her next five.

"All right, Maxine!" Ray yelled.

MAXINE

"About time. Don't count on Maxine if you plan to survive. Get up and start doing jumping jacks. When someone pukes, then we'll stop!" Mr. Idaho's voice was even harder.

Maxine felt like crying. She prayed it wouldn't be her that vomited. She stared at the clock keeping herself focused. Sweat trickled down her legs and gave her the shivers. Down the line, the sound of liquid hitting the floor relieved Maxine.

"All right, I see someone finally puked! Go to the back wall and brace yourself what's going to happen next!" The normally sedate gym teacher rubbed his hands together in excitement.

The group panted like a loud pack of wild dogs as they ran to the back wall. Maxine wiped sweat from her brow and rubbed it on her skirt. She made a mental note not to wear a sweater on detention day again. She noticed the only person not sweating and panting was Greg Maryland. He looked more content than miserable. Before she had a chance to assess the rest of the group a red rubber ball flew past her head.

"What the heck?!" A freshman girl yelled as a

red rubber ball smacked her in the leg. The balls were coming faster. At the other end of the basketball court, Mr. Idaho and Ray were loading red rubber balls into a launcher.

Mr. Idaho yelled, "Do you think you can run and hide now? Who's going to save you?" There was a certain glee to his voice, "You better learn to protect yourself if you can't follow the rules of McCarthy!"

Balls continued to fly, and no matter how fast Maxine tried to avert them, the other kids were faster. She caught two smaller students using her as a shield. If her mind wasn't so cloudy from exhaustion and confusion, she might have been offended, but she was looking for someone to be her shield.

Rob Illinois ended the misery for everyone with one single move. He stuck his hand up in the air and grabbed the ball coming at him.

"Bingo!" Mr. Idaho stopped feeding the machine. He smiled, "At least one of you would survive outside of here. The rest of you would be dead. Think about that. Let's go back to the room."

The footage continued. Scene after scene of dead people walking and eating, human beings acting worse than the dead, and sad people trying to remember a world that no longer existed.

In the final footage of the day, Rothgen militants cleaned up the streets and rescued people from buildings they had barricaded themselves into. Some of the survivors were so thin and dirty that they were carried out by people who wore protective yellow suits to keep from touching them.

In the background, other members of the group were shooting the few remaining dead, while a gurney carrying an emaciated woman was brought out of a building. The woman's eyes appeared empty and vacant as if there were no hope left inside of her. She didn't even appear relieved.

Max's brain was so exhausted from the sadness and depravity that she wanted to close her eyes here at the last moment. But then, suddenly, over the shoulder of one of the guards and right behind the tank, Max saw it: a shadow was running out from the side of the building.

It wasn't the dead; they couldn't move that fast.

It was someone living.

The person ran down the street, and out of nowhere, a guard popped out from a building and shot him. There were no fist pumping like before with the guy with the piercings. This was a trained person who shot people because that was what he did.

Max noticed how the camera was meant to keep your eye on the sickly women and children being pulled out of the building. Why was the man running? Didn't he want to be saved by Rothgen?

When the credits rolled, the Rothgen employees who helped collect the video footage were acknowledged. Mr. Idaho walked to the front of the room and flipped the lights on.

"All right everybody, move it. Back outside!" Mr. Idaho said. His eyes were bright and wide, giving him the appearance of maniacal joy.

Muscle fatigue overwhelmed Max. She didn't want to find out what other things Mr. Idaho did in detention that made him appear to be so alive.

The final indignation of the day was Mr. Idaho

chasing the group on a motorized cart around the outdoor track playing a game he called, Zombie Tag. The rules consisted of Mr. Idaho swatting students with a long measuring stick that he called the "zombie bite." Every time Maxine thought she might pass another student and get away, Mr. Idaho sped up, she'd fall back, and the cold hard smack of the stick would find her. She'd never sweated this much in her life.

After their fifteenth lap, Mr. Idaho pulled ahead of the pack and halted the runners. If Maxine had thought the group was panting like a group of wild dogs before, she wasn't sure what they were panting like now. Their breath was visible now as the fall sun began to decline in the sky. Now that Maxine was standing still, the sweat and cold made her legs feel like ice blocks. Max bent over, trying to put her head between her legs as best she could to catch her breath. Bending over had never been an easy thing for her.

"Okay, so can anyone tell me one of the rules we have in place to prevent something you saw in the videos?" Mr. Idaho asked.

"No guns," panted a boy behind Max.

Mr. Idaho nodded.

"No cars unless it is deemed necessary by the community for needs related to the community," said George Dakota.

"No aggression will be tolerated against another, nor will retaliation toward the aggressor," Greg Maryland said. He winked at Maxine.

Sue York pointed out, "Everything is provided by Rothgen so we don't have the crazy desires the freaks looting the stores were having. And: they protect us."

Max thought about Sue's comment for a minute. What kind of world would it be if everyone wore so many unique things? Would it really make people as crazy as those guys?

Mr. Idaho scanned the group. "Good job. If you are finishing your punishment today, try to stay out of trouble. If not, see you next week. You're excused."

Max stood bent over for a minute, trying to take in all that she'd been exposed to. She actually felt a little dizzy. Ray walked over to her and placed his hand on her back.

"Hey, I know it's a little much the first time, but after a while, it doesn't really affect you anymore. You'll become more physically fit, and the gruesome videos become less difficult to watch. Almost all of those people are dead. Their suffering is over. Let's get out of here."

Ray tugged at Max's sweater. She felt it all the way down to her toes.

Maxine shivered as they headed toward her home. Ray handed Max his coat. She looked at the ground, unsure of how to respond to someone offering her their coat. She was flattered, but also embarrassed. Her clothes were drenched in sweat.

They walked in the direction of her house in silence for a while, but then Ray asked, "Do you ever wonder what it would have been like before the war?"

Max was unsure of what to say. Her brain was exhausted after watching all the shock videos and running around like a crazed woman.

"I used to wonder a lot," said Ray. "I've seen all the videos. What would it be like to live in a big city? Choose your own profession, clothes, who you will date?"

"Why who you will date?" Max asked. "I didn't realize Rothgen could force you to date anyone."

Ray shoved his hands in his pockets. "If your father is the prestigious Dr. Pennsylvania, then yes, you can be told who to date."

"Oh," Max said. She didn't want to ruin it with him already, but now that he'd admitted Dr. Pennsylvania was his father, she really wanted to ask about Ellen.

Instead, she decided talk about the films. "Why do you think they make us watch these films in detention?"

He scoffed. "Really? Are you trying to be cute and dumb? Or are you for real?"

She stared at him, taken aback. No one have ever accused her of being dumb or cute.

He stopped walking and turned to her. "Those videos are meant to scare you into believing that these communities are the best way to live. The only way to live. Obey, repress your urges, allow yourself to be controlled."

He gently stroked her face. All the blood left her head. He pulled away.

Max was silent. She trudged behind him. How could she argue with Ray? She didn't know anything, except that something was growing inside of her that she couldn't control. Whatever that thing was, it didn't like authority or her repressing her feelings. It didn't want to be controlled.

They were two blocks from Max's house when Ray stopped at a corner and pointed. "See the tree line?"

Max nodded as she looked out past several streets of houses. In the distance, row after row of trees fell behind the line.

"Have you ever wondered what's behind those trees?" he questioned.

Max shook her head no. She felt sheepish. There had never been a reason to know what was behind the tree line.

"Behind that line is a concrete fence that is thick enough that men with guns walk back and forth across it day and night. They have silencers on their guns so that people can't hear them go off. Why do they have that if we are all safe? If Rothgen saved the world, then what are we being protected against? We were told all guns were eliminated. Those are guns. Guns just like the ones in the videos." Ray's face filled with color as his voice was laced with venom.

"How do you know? Did you go out there and see these guys walking around up on this fence?" Max asked as they started walking toward her street.

"Yeah, I went out there. The first time it was by accident. I was looking for something else and crossed past the markers. I kept going. I heard some people talking and followed their voices. That's when I saw the fence and the guys up top. I couldn't hear what they were saying, but they watch the perimeter all the time. The Rothgen Army is always waiting and watching." Ray stopped at the walkway leading up to Maxine's front door.

"Thanks for walking me home." Max looked up into Ray's eyes. It wasn't a date, and he wasn't her boyfriend, but part of her wanted a farewell kiss. Ray crossed his arms.

"No problem. I've been hoping to talk to you since I learned about your stellar academic record. You're a lot different than the other girls," Ray said. Then he continued. "You have a long way to go to actually know anything, instead of regurgitating words back to the teachers."

"How did you know who I was? Do they put us on display for student teachers?" Max asked.

"Everyone knows you. You think only the top ten smart kids care about rank? Everyone cares about the rank. There's nothing else to measure our lives by. We are all ranked in importance in some way whether it is in school or in the community in general."

Ray relaxed his arms as Max stepped away. She turned to head toward the house, but her desire to know what had happened to his sister stopped her.

"What happened to Ellen? Where did she go? Why are people pretending like she didn't exist?" Max asked quickly. She hoped that throwing the questions out there all at once would catch him off-guard and he would talk to her.

Ray's face transformed from that of someone who felt a connection and kinship with Max into a blank, cold face that didn't know her at all. When he spoke again, his voice sounded void of humanity and the fire that seemed to ignite him.

"I don't have a sister," Ray said.

"Oh, I thought you were Dr. Pennsylvania's son. Dr. Penn had a daughter named Ellen. She hasn't been to school in a week." Max felt herself apologizing. She needed to bring back the Ray she'd exchanged glances with the entire afternoon.

"I am Dr. Penn's son. His only child. There is no Ellen."

Ray backed up. To Max, he looked like a small animal being cornered by a predator. It was not the reaction she'd expected. Ray opened his mouth as though he were going to say something else, then closed it, turned around, and walked away.

"Wait! I'm sorry. I didn't mean to upset you!" Max yelled after him. Ray waved his left hand up in the air, saluting goodbye. The frustration of losing that amazing feeling of flirtation, excitement, and miniscule amount of affection thwarted Max into desperation.

Her fingernails felt like they were going to pop off the tips of her fingers, her breathing increased, and the blood coursing through her veins burned like acid. The squeaking of her teeth grinding against one another was maddening. She felt her nostrils flaring with each labored breath. Her stomach burned and ached.

If she let it get too far, she might do something she didn't want to, and she couldn't chance that again. Her best bet was to run to her bedroom and hide until it passed.

CHAPTER 6

"How'd it go?" Dr. Penn's voice asked through the phone.

Rob Massachusetts held the handset away from his ear. Dr. Penn's voice sounded like gravel being thrown in a garbage disposal to him right about now. He couldn't stand the guy.

"If you're asking if he had sex with my daughter on the way home from school, I think the answer is no," Rob said dryly.

"Well, I don't think that is going to happen with her. She is most likely going to be triggered from her encounter with him in general. Has she been aggressive or shown any more violence?"

"What does *triggered* exactly mean?" Rob asked. He looked up at the ceiling. Thumps and crashes abounded above him.

"The metamorphosis," Dr. Penn sighed. "Just keep her door locked. There is no telling if she'll turn out like the rest or not."

"Will do." Rob hung up the phone. He looked over at his wife, who sat on their polyester couch, staring vacantly into space.

Before Rob could open his mouth, Erin said, "I would give anything for a gin and tonic. Of all the rules in this place, you'd think they'd at least give us some booze."

Rob walked over to the couch and sat down next to Erin. He grabbed her hand and squeezed tightly. It was quiet for a moment. Then the sounds of shattering glass, thumps, and bumps began again.

"Here, put this away." Erin handed Rob the handgun.

Rob took it from her, then handed her the newspaper. He walked over to the fireplace, pulled back the cookie-cutter painting that was the same as the one over every mantle in every house in the community, and placed the gun in the safe that were like every other gun and safe, in every other house in the community.

"Would you like some ice tea, dear?" Rob asked.

"Yes, please."

CHANGES

Max opened her eyes, rolled over, and wiped the drool from her cheek. Her regulation, frilly white comforter lay next to her on the floor, several of her drawers were strewn out across the room with clothes lying everywhere, and it looked as though she had bitten herself on the forearm.

Max picked herself up off the plush carpet and started putting away her disaster. She hoped her parents had not walked in and witnessed the event. What was causing the extreme rush of anger? Why did she forget who she was when the feeling took over?

MAXINE

After an hour of folding up clothes, putting away papers, and finally making her bed, the room was back to regulation standards. It was Saturday evening. While other kids were out having social time at the bowling alley or volunteering to promote Rothgen community service goals, she lay in her bed, staring at the ceiling and thinking about the new guy she'd met, liked, and lost in a matter of five hours.

Ray Pennsylvania's paleness was not a sign of goodness, but a signifier that he was on the edge of darkness. He saw the world in a way she hadn't even thought of yet. She knew that he knew what had happened to Ellen. She felt it in her gut. If she didn't see him again all week, she'd bide her time until detention.

Ray had Max's attention, but Nathan Nevada was still on her mind. Why had he complimented her this afternoon? Was it to get her heart rate elevated? Had he scuffed her shoe to get her in trouble? Her heart always raced at his attention or touch.

Max wasn't stupid. She knew Nathan was aware

that she had a crush on him. It was the most likely reason he tormented her so much. There were loads of girls in the school who liked him. She knew for a fact that snarky, hateful Esther Hampshire would die if he walked her home from school. Esther was pretty, too. She had big blue eyes that sparkled mischievously when she was about to tear someone apart, and her hair was a beautiful reddish brown.

Max remembered the paper wad Nathan had thrown at her head earlier in the week. She'd stuffed it under the bed to hide from her mother. She rolled onto the floor, sliding her hand under the bed to grab it. She felt up and down in the area she remembered leaving it. Finally she lifted the bed skirt, looking for the paper. Empty. Max panicked. Had her mother grabbed it? Where could it be? Had there really been an inspection?

Max ran downstairs to find her mother and father sitting in the living room, reading.

Max's mother looked up from her copy of *Rothgen's Guide to Good Housekeeping* with concern. "Are you okay?"

"Did you clean my room?" Max asked.

"No, that's your job," her mother said. Then she questioned, "What's wrong? Did the inspectors actually *take* something? From what I understand, if they take something they have to write it down on our checklist."

Max stared blankly at her mother.

"Max, you're scaring me."

Her mother looked to Max's father with concern. Then her father spoke. "Are you okay?"

"I'm fine. I just didn't believe anyone really inspected our house. That's all."

Max felt hollow inside. Her father left the door unlocked on Saturday afternoons so that the inspectors could come in and ensure that everything was up to regulation code and there was no contraband. She had known this since she was a small girl. She had never believed it was true. Nothing had ever been moved or taken out of place. She hadn't even known there was a checklist that her parents were given, stating they'd had the inspection.

Her father looked at her jokingly. "Max, did you really think we made that up to get you to do your chores? It's part of the pact we signed."

Max had never worried about breaking rules or regulations, but now it seemed she was ending up on the wrong side of *all* of them, and it scared the hell out of her. The life they lived in the community was real. The rules were real, and you weren't supposed to break them. And, now an important secret could be exposed.

Someone had taken the note from Nathan.

Rothgen girls should always try to get along. If your personality doesn't seem to agree with the crowd, you might want to change it.

CHAPTER 7

"You warned her?!" Ray asked. He combed his fingers through his jet black hair. "You want *all* of us to die, or just *your* dumb ass?"

Nathan leaned against the counter. "You afraid if she knows what you sickos have in store for her, she'll run off?"

"It's natural selection. You think you genetically-blessed pretty boys are the only ones that have a desire to survive? We're a new race of humans, and eventually, we'll be our own species." Ray grinned. "The virus will make sure of it."

"Do you hold on to that? Does it make you feel

better to know you're a weapon for Rothgen? People here are like sheep. They file one by one to the slaughterhouse if told to." Nathan stared at Ray as though he were a bug.

This seemed to make Ray laugh more. He picked up a beaker and rolled the base in the palm of his hand. "Ah, poor little brother. Had to see your big sis cut down by the Suits. The weak ones will fail and the strong will prevail."

Nathan stood up straight. "She wasn't weak. She was sick. Just like you, just like Maxine."

Ray leaned in. "Well, we all know what your sister did."

Nathan walked toward the door. "We all know what *you* did to your *sister*."

Ray calmly said, "She was a casualty of war. Simple."

"Keep telling yourself that. It will keep the guilt down." Nathan slammed the door behind him.

Ray stayed for a moment, anger, frustration, and immense guilt flooding him at the thought of his sister. He slammed the beaker on the marble counter. Fine cracks edged up through the glass.

BAD GIRLS HAVE ALL THE FUN

Silence pressurized the hallways, making Max feel as though every movement required extra effort. She looked up at the round wall clock; it read seven a.m. She had snuck in the side door to the cafeteria when the lunch ladies weren't looking. If she was caught in the building without going through the proper procedure, she'd end up with more detention. Not that it mattered. She had a goal: find Ray Pennsylvania.

Her Sunday had been spent analyzing every

word and movement she'd made since meeting him. She wanted that amazing feeling of connection back. The air felt easier to breathe when she talked to him. She didn't worry that her veins would creep out or that her skin was too white. The two contrasted the perfection that surrounded them in unity. Her only problem was: she didn't know where to find him.

Thoughts of Nathan rolled her stomach. She wondered if he would talk about what was on the paper wad. Most likely he would ignore her as usual, or embarrass her again. Which led her to another problem: an inspector had her note.

She didn't know who the home inspectors were. Who did they report to in the community? The Suits? Lately, Max felt like the most ignorant person in McCarthy. There were no answers to questions that should have been asked long before she'd allowed the school to slip an ankle bracelet on her.

Max shook off the failure of not knowing her world and started thinking of where Ray would spend his time during the school day. Where would he be assigned as a student teacher? All students had to go through the security process before entering the school. Did student teachers?

She eyed the vacant table and chairs in the lobby. She could casually sit there and pretend to read a book while waiting for him. She walked onward. As she passed each classroom, rows of empty seats became a haze.

Before detention, fear and insecurity had gnawed at Max when others students looked like they might bump her from her rank. *It's liberating being a zero*, thought Max. No pressure to read the chapters, worry about the test, or whether she made the teacher happy.

Max came upon the chemistry lab. She liked this room best. Life was created out of chemistry. Every molecule of the body was fused together through the elements, just like everything else on Earth.

It made her feel equal to everyone else. They were all made of carbon, oxygen, sodium, calcium, and hydrogen. None of the beautiful, strong people could refute that she was made from the same things as them. She felt drawn to enter the room.

When she quietly opened the door, she heard them immediately: voices arguing in the chemical closet, loudly enough to be heard over the din of three ventilations hoods. It sounded like a heated discussion between two males, but their voices were muted.

She wanted to go peek through the closet door's window, but the door was at the back of the room, and there'd be no time to hide if one of the men opened it. As she stood debating, the doorknob turned. Max backed out of the room, looking both ways. The only place she could hide was at the water fountain at the end of the hallway.

She ran quickly to the fountain, her loafers sliding on the laminate floor as she landed. She let the cool water hit her mouth, but tried to look in the direction of the lab to see who'd been arguing. The first person to come out of the room was Nathan, and behind him, to her surprise, was Ray.

She kept her head down, trying not to choke down the water. The boys continued talking and turned to the right, heading away from her. She wasn't sure whether they saw her. How did the two know each other? Why would they argue in private during school hours? As they turned the corner, Max followed.

The boys split up in the lobby: Ray walked out of the school and Nathan headed toward his locker. He passed by Maxine, avoiding her presence.

Before she lost her courage, she ran after him, yelling, "Wait! I need to talk to you!" He continued ignoring her. The other students started filing into the school. It was becoming crowded. Her pulse rose, and desperation flooded her.

"I said, I need to talk to you. Don't pretend like I don't exist!" Max said. The growl in her voice attracted his attention. He turned to her.

"Is there something I can help you with, Max-een?" Nathan said.

"Yeah." She marched toward him. Her heartbeat continued to rise. "I want to know why you gave me that message. Why do you think I am going to end up dead?"

"I have no idea what you're talking about," he said. His face was blank, and his voice monotone.

123

MAXINE

Desperation turned to anger. Everyone was hiding things from her, pretending as though she wasn't strong enough to handle the truth, or couldn't be trusted. Without thinking, she lunged forward on tiptoe and grabbed the collar of Nathan's favorite cornflower blue shirt. His eyes widened.

"I'm sick of this. You know what? I don't have a damn clue what happened, but people are pretending like Ellen Penn isn't gone, including her own brother. You send me a passive-aggressive message warning me that I am going to die and expect me not to get upset?"

Max paused when Nathan pulled her hands from his collar. He gripped her pudgy hands in his and looked into her eyes. He pulled her close.

"You're making a scene," Nathan said. "Do you have a death wish? Look around you."

Max took a deep breath as she felt his warm body close to hers. She surveyed the hallway. She didn't see anything out of the ordinary. Teachers scanned students' ankle bracelets as they came into the school; Mr. Oregon walked around discouraging loiterers.

"All of these adults, they have many purposes in our lives. They do more than teach here. I suggest you calm down. I'll talk to you after school." Nathan released her hands.

Her body slowed, but her anger at being manipulated and patronized stayed. She composed herself. "Okay." Then, without thinking, she swiftly kicked Nathan Nevada in the shin. He bent over and rubbed it.

"What was *that* for?" he asked.

"I'm sick of being messed with by everyone— you, my parents, the glowing girls, and this stupid school. Tell Ray Penn I have got one for him, too." Max walked away.

She wasn't a baby, but if they wanted to treat her like a little girl, she was going to give them a taste of what that was going to be like. Max felt her spine straighten as she walked away. Mr. Oregon glared as she passed him by. She held her head high as she walked to homeroom. She would not be pushed around anymore.

A temper was supposed to be a bad thing, but

Max wasn't so sure. She needed that fire to keep her going.

She wasn't the last student into homeroom today, but she still chose to sit up front. She looked ahead, unworried about passing out papers and standing out. Ms. Maine stood at the front of the room and smiled at Max.

"Maxine, I'm glad to see you're willing to take on more leadership. It's a good way to get your rank back up," Ms. Maine said, handing the morning announcements to Maxine. Max tugged hard at the papers and rolled her eyes. She stood up.

"Whatever. I'm sick of hiding." Max looked at the students in front of her. She drew a deep breath and exhaled. She needed to make it through the day to find out what Nathan and Ray had fought about.

She counted papers for the first row and thrust the stack at a broad-shouldered rugby player who'd called her "Fatts-a-shits-itts" one too many times. She bumped the edge of his desk with her stomach. He looked at her, puzzled.

Each front row student received a little of her

wrath. One after another, she bumped them, breathed heavily on purpose, and looked them all directly in the eyes. When she finished her task, she sat down, waiting for the morning pledges and reminders of restrictions.

As Mr. Oregon's voice droned on, Max studied the picture of the Rothman family at the front of the classroom. Everyone in the family had the same smile, the same eyes. They seemed unfazed by the war.

Almost every adult Max knew had a dead look in their eyes the minute they thought no one was watching. Where did their sadness go?

The clang of the morning bell interrupted her thoughts. She headed out the door and pushed herself into the crowd of students. The old Max would have waited for everyone else to the leave the room, but the crowd exhilarated her now. She shoved forward.

The glowing girls paraded around in their high-waisted white cotton commissary underwear through the rows of lockers and benches, to show the rest of the girls what a fine specimen of young womanhood should look like.

At sixteen, they all had rounded breasts, tiny waists, and beautifully curved hips. The sight of them normally upset Max, but today, as Esther Hampshire flaunted her body in front of the less-developed girls, Max felt shameless.

Max opened her locker, pulling out her freshly-washed gym clothes. She slid off her black cotton sweater and slipped her grey regulation t-shirt over her head.

For a minute, nothing seemed wrong.

She wiggled out of her skirt, folded it, and placed it in the locker. She bent down to slip on her gym shorts. She stopped. Something wasn't right.

The extra-large shirt felt loose across her chest. No piece of clothing had ever felt loose on her. She hoisted the shorts up and slipped into her gym shoes. Nonchalantly, she walked over to the mirrors.

It wasn't imaginary: her shirt was loose. Had it stretched since the last time she'd worn it? The fullness of the arm holes made her think not.

"When did you start caring about your looks?" Esther purred behind her.

"I need to go," she mumbled. It had only been four periods since homeroom—when she decided to kick ass. She was backing down already. Shame engulfed her. The glowing girls sensed her weakness. Their senses reminded her of a Geiger counter waving over every girl, looking for their most damaged spot.

She pursed her lips, holding back the hateful words that wanted to spew forth. Her desire to speak to Nathan overrode her desire to smart off to Esther. She walked away.

Fingernails dug into her arm as she passed through the doorway leading to the gym.

"Where are you going?" Nancy Oregon said. "She asked you a question." Her grip tightened on Maxine. Nancy's eyes lit up with excitement, and she curled her nails deeper into Max's flesh.

There was no stopping it. The tidal wave of rage fell over Max.

"Get your hand off me or I'll rip your arm off and feed it to you," Max spat at her.

MAXINE

Nancy turned away from the spit and laughed. "Mess-a-shit-etts, you're hilarious."

Max growled. In the back of her mind she screamed. Then she blacked out.

CHAPTER 8

"Leave her alone!"

The phrase rang through Nathan's head. Some nights it was so loud and lasted so long that he rolled over and covered his ears with his pillow, trying to dampen it. If the visions of his sister Melissa came with it, he let the tears roll.

Tonight, he laid in bed with his arms crossed under his head and stared at the ceiling, remembering her. She was older, but like him, otherwise: tall, athletic, and blonde. Her laugh was light and airy, and she loved to laugh.

He closed his eyes, wanting to remember when

they'd played blocks for a whole day one time when he was four. Instead, the screamed phrase rang through his ears, and now the bad memories came.

It had started with the bronze door knocker clanging back and forth. The sound had startled him from the living room floor, where he'd been laying on his stomach, writing his spelling words. He'd wanted to answer the door, but his Mom had told him he wasn't old enough. He'd ignored the knocks, and had continued to spell his words. C-a-t, c-a-t, b-a-t; he'd written them over and over. The doorbell had rang again. He'd stood up to answer. Whoever had at the door had been impatient.

"I'll be right there!" his mother had yelled from the kitchen. Nathan had sat back down and began writing again. B-a-t, h-a-t, h-a-t, r-a-t, r-a-t. The door had opened.

"Hello?"

Nathan had looked up to see the mailman peeking his head through the door. "Mrs. Nevada? I need to deliver something to you."

"Melissa, can you help him?" Mrs. Nevada had

yelled.

"I have it, Mom!" Nathan had yelled as he'd jumped up to grab the package. He'd wanted to show he was just as responsible as Melissa.

"Where's your Mom?" The mailman had smiled, showing his teeth.

Nathan had frowned at him. He hadn't been the normal guy. "Where's Mr. Kentucky?"

"He went to a special place. Go get your Mom." The mailman had pushed himself into the entryway.

"Mom!" Nathan yelled.

"Where's Melissa?" Mrs. Nevada had yelled back. She'd walked out of the kitchen. Her hands had been raised in the air, coated with bloody crackers and ground meat. She'd stopped when she'd seen the mailman.

"Who are you?"

"Mrs. Nevada?" The mailman had stood up straighter. Nathan had noticed he didn't have a package for them.

Nathan had heard the thumps of Melissa running toward the stairs. He'd looked at his mother, then the man. They'd both shifted their gazes toward the stairs. The mailman had opened his side bag.

"Mom, do you need me?" Melissa had asked as she hit the stairs.

Mrs. Nevada had let out a primal scream.

Nathan had froze. He'd never heard a sound like what had come out of his mother's mouth. The mailman had pulled a black object from his bag and aimed it at his sister. The sound of firecrackers had filled the room. Mrs. Nevada had lunged toward the man as Melissa had toppled down the stairs.

Nathan's fear had evaporated and he ran toward the mailman, too. He'd kicked and screamed and yelled, "Leave her alone!" until he'd been hoarse. The last thing he remembered before a fist came in contact with his face was bloody crackers and ground meat on the white canvas pants of the man.

When he'd regained consciousness, he found he'd instinctually curled into a ball. He'd sat up. It'd been night. The light from outside illuminated a large black pool of liquid that ran from the staircase landing to the entryway. It had been smeared all the way to the door.

He'd looked for his mother. In the living room he'd seen a shape and walked toward it.

"Mom?" Nathan had asked as he crept past the matching flowered chairs that he wasn't allowed to sit in. He'd walked over to her. Her apron was covered in black. He'd poked her.

"Hmmm?" she'd mumbled.

"Where's Melissa?" he'd asked.

"She's gone," Mrs. Nevada had said.

"What do you mean, Momma?" He'd crawled into her lap, hoping she'd wrap him in her arms. They'd stayed limp by her sides.

He'd lain his head on her chest. The dried black substance on her apron had scratched his face. He hadn't been sure what to do. His Mom had never been this sleepy. He'd closed his eyes and cried.

Now he was sixteen, and the man of the house when his father was out on the road. He couldn't cry. All he could do was stare at the ceiling and try to help Maxine not end up dead.

YOU ONLY HURT THE ONES YOU LOVE

The concrete floor felt cool against her face. Her eyes fluttered as the sound of shoes shuffled around her. Max attempted to push herself up, but met resistance in the middle of her back.

"Hold on, Maxine. Don't try to get up too fast. Your friends said you fell and hit your head." The firm hands gently guided her onto her back. A round face with soft eyes greeted her.

Ms. Texas had been the school nurse since the establishment of the community. It was odd: there were few women like Ms. Texas and Ms. Maine, those who chose work over children and marriage. Though she had a youthful glow to her, the soft lines around her eyes and the sadness behind them made Max believe she was much older than she appeared.

Behind Ms. Texas, the glowing girls stood back against the wall, staring at Max. Nancy Oregon's eyes were filled with tears and terror. She cradled one hand delicately in the other, blood flowing through her fingers and dripping to the floor.

When Max looked directly at her, Nancy turned her face away. Max smiled. Nancy would never lay another hand on her. Ms. Texas put out her hand to help Max up.

"Max, have you had a seizure before? Do you know what those are?" Ms. Texas asked.

"No, I don't have seizures. I just blanked out," Max responded.

"Well, from what the girls tell me, it sounds like you had a seizure. You lost control of your body and started trembling. You tried to lunge at Nancy, and bit her. What made you do that?" Ms. Texas asked. She spoke directly and matter-of-fact. She pulled Max the rest of the way up and helped steady her. "Let's go to the nursing station. I'll look at Nancy's hand and call both your parents. The rest of you can go to gym."

Esther protested, "I don't want to leave Nancy alone with Max. She's dangerous."

Ms. Texas nodded, acknowledging Esther. "I understand your concern, but both girls will be fine, and no one is in any danger. Believe me."

Esther mumbled something under her breath. Policy dictated that children follow adult instruction at all times, unless they wanted to be penalized. Esther scuttled to the gymnasium. Marie and Karlene followed behind her like two little ducklings following after their mother. Through her haze, Max recalled a book from elementary school about ducklings and their Mom.

Nancy leaned against the wall. She wouldn't move until Ms. Texas instructed her to do so.

"Let's go, Nancy. We need to make sure you're okay. I'm sure your Dad will be proud that you tried to help a fellow student when she was so vulnerable."

Ms. Texas smiled at Nancy. Max looked at Nancy from behind Ms. Texas' arm. She raised an eyebrow at Nancy. Her intention was to let Nancy know Max was aware that she hadn't been helping her when Max had blacked out. Nancy shuddered, and smiled weakly.

"I try to do my best at all times. I'm the principal's daughter. I've got to be a good example."

Max held back a laugh. It was the kind that developed from noxious air instead of joy-filled oxygen. It was acrid and smothering, but she shoved it back down her throat. She didn't want Ms. Texas to lose empathy for her. Max knew now that she had tried to defend herself while in the fugue state. Nancy was lucky that she had just bitten her. She'd meant every word she'd said before she'd blacked out. She really would've ripped Nancy's arm off.

The three walked out of the locker room and toward the nurses' station. The hallway was quiet except for the voice of instruction as they passed each class. Max missed the part of herself that lived for the moments in class when she held her hand up, knowing every answer.

Now she was a zero, an aggressor, a one hundred-and-eighty-five-pound fireball who kicked cute boys and had the guts to go after the one she wanted.

Now that she thought about it, maybe she *hated* being a know-it-all.

Besides, what did she really know? She didn't know a damn thing about her body. The policies and rules that regulated every movement of her life were slowly killing her and the rest of her classmates. Until Ray had pointed it out on Saturday, she hadn't known there was a fence guarded by Rothgen men with guns ready to fire on those who wanted to come in or leave.

By the time they were old enough to graduate, what would be left for them? The girls would get married and have children. She would sit at home like her mother. She would cook, clean, and nurture other little human beings to follow policies and procedures. Was this what her life was about?

Being subservient to beautiful people and a corporation that had allegedly saved her unborn life?

The hall began to narrow and widen—at least, in Max's vision it appeared that way. Her breathing quickened, her heart raced, and she gasped as she felt the now-familiar out-of-control sensation go through her again. "No, no, no."

Ms. Texas started to lean in toward her. She felt her head instinctually leaning toward Ms. Texas' outreached hand. Max's teeth were exposed.

"These are the worst seizures I've ever seen," Ms. Texas said. She braced herself, ready to catch Max. As Max's vision blurred, she saw someone push Ms. Texas out of the way. Blonde wavy hair was the last thing Maxine saw before she felt a sharp sear at her jawline.

"Afflicted girl, wake up." She felt cold hands tap on her cheeks. This had been her second violent episode in one day. Exhausted, opening her eyes seemed a monumental task.

"No, I'm going to sleep for the rest of my life," she said, rolling away from the prickly fingers.

"Max, you gotta get the hell up before Principal Oregon is allowed in here. He is ready to put you down himself for biting Nancy. You've become the rebel of Rothgen High. You're not safe. We gotta get out of here before the Suits are called in."

The idea of the Suits scared Max awake. She worried they were waiting for justification to pull her away from her family. She opened her eyes and rolled over. As she turned towards the boy's voice, she hoped it belonged to the one guy who made her feel less like a freak. Her heart sunk as she saw Nathan, and not Ray.

As she came back to life, she realized that her jaw was heavy on the right side, and piercing pain shot through her with each movement of her mouth.

"Why did you hit me?" she asked.

"Because, you were going to bite Ms. Texas. What is about to happen to Nancy is not going to be good," he said, his lips set in a straight line. There was neither a frown nor a cocky smile behind it. He wasn't joking, or picking on her.

"Max," he said, "I sent you that message for a

reason. It's no joke. You're changing. If we don't get a plan in place for you, they will make you disappear. Your Dad's position is the only thing letting you stay."

Max was about to ask a question when the door opened. Ms. Texas came in.

"Nathan Nevada, I told you to stay on your side of the divider. What is *wrong* with you children? Don't you understand orders anymore? It's like there is some kind of anarchy virus surging through your little hormonal heads." She pointed toward the other side of the divider. "Get over there and don't touch Max again. Understand?"

"I'm sorry, Ms. T. I just wanted to make sure she didn't have another seizure," Nathan said. He lowered his shoulders in a non-threatening manner, and moved to the other side.

Ms. Texas continued to talk. "I know you thought you were helping her, but really? Punching someone who was having a seizure? She wasn't going to hurt me. I'm just surprised. They're going to send you to the medical center after Mr. Oregon talks to you, Max. Dr. Pennsylvania wants to examine you and run some tests."

The door swung open before Ms. Texas could finish. Max's Mom came in.

"I'm here to get Max. We'll take her to the doctor in the morning," Her mother said. "I already cleared it with Dr. Pennsylvania."

"That's odd. I've been instructed to keep her here until they bring the van to pick her up. I talked to Dr. Penn myself," Ms. Texas said, folding her arms across her chest.

Max's mom squinted, her face flushed. The auburn highlights in her hair seemed to shine more brightly. Her green eyes pierced Ms. Texas.

"Gretchen," she said, "I'm sure a smart working girl like yourself understands a mother's desire to have her child at home in her bed instead of a scary, cold hospital. Dr. Pennsylvania understood that when my husband called him."

Max's Mom came over and sat on the edge of her bed. She looked at Max. Her eyes were cold, clinical, calculating, and there was no warmth in them. It was worse than the look Max had seen in her the night her Mom had traced the pattern of the wallpaper in the dining room while her Dad scolded her.

Max sat up immediately. She didn't think now was the time to argue with her mother, and of the two options, going with her mother seemed better than being around Dr. Penn.

"Ms. T, I think I'm good," Nathan said. "I'll walk Mrs. Massachusetts and Max home, if that's okay with you." Through the curtain, Max saw that the tension in his shoulders was back.

Before Ms. T could talk, Max's mother said, "Don't worry about us, Nathan. We'll be fine. I used to be a nurse. I can handle any kind of seizure."

Max heard it in her mother's voice. She didn't think Max had had a seizure. But if that wasn't what was wrong with her, then what was it?

Max stood up to grab her coat. It would be cool outside, and her legs were bare. As she put it on, she noticed her Mom looking at her body.

There was no more matter-of-fact terminology about body development, no quirky nurse to talk about puberty. Her mother just had some kind of

146

sad, remorseful look at the sight of Max's shirt loosened in the stomach and tightened in the chest.

She turned away and instructed Max, "Let's go."

Max followed with her head down. She felt ashamed of her actions and her body now. Her mother—a woman who loved biology and never made the human body seem freakish—had made her feel disgusting and gross with just one look.

The two headed toward the front of the building. Max's mother charged forward with a determined look on her face. Max had trouble keeping up with her. Her lungs burned as her loafers clicked in double time to keep up with her mother's stride. At the front of the building stood Principal Oregon, his arms crossed and his body held solid as a barrier between the two women and the doors.

"Max isn't leaving this building until I talk to her about her actions today," Mr. Oregon said. His voice was stern. "She hurt Nancy. If Nancy is going to the medical center to be evaluated, so is Max."

"Max is going home," her mother said. She slowed her pace as she came closer to Principal

Oregon. "If Nancy and her little buddies would keep their hands to themselves and their mouths shut, these things wouldn't happen." Max's Mom stopped, crossed her arms, and looked up at Mr. Oregon, challenging him.

"Your daughter is *changing*. And now, Nancy will too…" Mr. Oregon stopped and looked past Max and her Mom.

"What're they doing?" he asked. Max and her Mom turned around to see a shadow running down the hall.

The siren went off with a startling shriek. Max covered her ears. Mr. Oregon ran in the direction Max and her Mom had come from.

Max's Mom grabbed her arm and pulled her out the front doors. Her Mom didn't hesitate. She never looked back to see if Mr. Oregon noticed. Max figured it was something left over from the war.

Never look back and never regret, Max thought. She remembered her mother saying it over and over, when she told stories of the war. Now, she saw what that meant to her mother: it meant taking opportunities when they were presented, and moving forward.

When they were three blocks from the school, her mother's pace finally slowed. Her breathing eased. Two fire trucks zoomed past them as they walked toward their house. A silver sedan drove toward the school at a lightning speed.

The Suits had been notified of the fire alarm.

Had Nathan triggered it? Why did he know so much about what was going on? She didn't know what was happening to her body, but *he* did? It infuriated her.

Her mother broke the silence. "I guess we need to order you new gym shirts and a better bra. That's usually how they come in. One minute you're running around free, nothing weighing you down, and then all of the sudden you've got a burden on your chest that will last a lifetime."

She still didn't look at Max. She looked off in the distance. It made Max feel alone and gross, whether her Mom meant to say it that way or not.

"Mom, I thought you said this was all normal and I shouldn't freak out about it when it happened?" Max asked.

She sighed. "I know honey. Nothing is happening the way I imagined it would."

The two walked in silence the rest of the way home. Cool wind burned Maxine's face, and dead leaves brushed her hair. Life was dying all around her while her body began to bloom.

As the two entered the house, they found Max's Dad sitting in the dark living room with his back to them. Slits of gold shined through the shades, radiating down on their standard-issue area rug. The outline of his head and shoulders was all that Max could see on the couch. She edged into the living room to talk to him.

"Max, go up to your room, shut the door, and don't come out until you're told. Understand?" Her father said.

His voice was different. He no longer sounded warm and loving. He used the same voice with her Mom. "Make sure she does what I say, then come back down here."

Max's mother didn't speak. She swallowed hard and looked at Max. Max didn't want the fear to show in her eyes. *Scared* could not compare to how she felt. Her parents were acting like they didn't know her anymore.

She wasn't their little girl. She was something else to them now. Her mother held her hand, but she didn't feel that psychic warm bond they had held so dearly even a week ago. The hand felt foreign. There was no squeeze of encouragement or mischief. It was just a hand as they walked up the stairs. Her mother guided her to her room, then let go of her to open the door for Max.

She pulled Max close to her and hugged her tight. Max felt something warm on top of her head. Then her mother kissed her forehead. "You'll always be my little girl."

She walked out of the room and shut the door. Max heard an unusual sound: a click, and a mechanical turn.

Her mother had locked her in the room.

There was no switch on Max's side of the door. She walked over to the bed, sat down, and rocked back and forth, comforting herself for a few minutes.

From where she sat, she could hear mumbling

downstairs. She walked over to the heating grate, hoping that the words would travel. Her parents had moved to the dining room. Max's bedroom sat directly above it. She pressed her ear as close to the floor as she possibly could, straining to hear every word.

"Look," Max's Dad said, "we reported it when we moved in. We signed the agreement form."

"No, *you* signed the damn form," her Mom said "*I* didn't. It's not her fault. They can't just get rid of her. I'm not stupid, and neither is Max. Apparently, neither is the Nevada boy. Luckily, I found the note before the inspectors did."

"We all know the Nevada boy knows what can happen," her Dad said, raising his voice "Why do you think they keep him front and center as a model teenager? They're watching and waiting for him to start doing something stupid. To act out."

"I won't let them do it. I won't. Do you remember how cold those bastards can be?" her Mom said.

"You want me to do it? Will that make you feel better, huh? Her own family does it? Do you *admire* Bradley Pennsylvania for the things he has done in the name of the community?" her Dad asked.

"Don't be like that. Brad did what he had to do. No one knew that could happen. Ellen was a tragedy. *It* was a tragedy. How do you think *Ray* feels about it? Do you think anyone would want that to happen to their sister?" Erin said.

"Max created one tragedy today," her father said. "It could have been two. She won't be able to control it." His voice sounded defeated.

There was a knock at the front door. Max heard footsteps. Then the sound of a gruff voice carried through the quiet house. The Suits had arrived; she could feel it. Max pushed herself up from the floor and sat cross-legged.

She awaited her fate.

CHAPTER 9

"Daddy, I don't want to go to the medical center," Nancy Oregon pouted. She crossed her arms, and flopped so hard on to the lime green couch that it shifted under the force of her tiny frame.

Mr. Oregon shoved Nancy's school books in her backpack. Then he scanned the living room, looking for anything else that she might need.

"Princess, you'll get to see Ellen again. She's been at the medical facility for a week now. I'm sure she'll be happy to see you." He softened his voice like he had when she was a little girl and he'd needed to coax her.

"But nobody talks about Ellen anymore. We have to pretend like she doesn't exist. Isn't that what you told me?" Her tone went from pouty and playful to serious.

"Yes, Ellen will no longer be a part of the McCarthy community. It is unfortunate but true." Mr. Oregon rubbed the bald spot on the top of his head.

"Will I get to come home again?" Nancy asked, her voice now soft. She stared down at her bandaged hand and picked at the gauze.

"Of course, darling, you are going in for treatment of a bite, nothing more. Go get your toothbrush so we can get moving," Mr. Oregon said, changing the subject. It was hard to lie to his only child. He didn't know if he would ever see her again.

But he'd been lying to Nancy since the day he'd spotted her in the back of a semi-truck full of orphans and misfits who'd been hauled into the community.

Like so many of the other children in McCarthy,

she'd been appointed to someone. He didn't know how the two-year-old had ended up alone. He just knew that if his partner William had made it, he'd have loved having such a cute daughter.

Instead, Mr. Oregon had had to lie. Tell Nancy about a mother that didn't exist, and pretend that he'd never had a husband who he'd loved more than anything.

Now, he was going to have to say goodbye to Nancy with the hope that she'd been born with the virus and would live through what was about to happen to her. They all knew that little shit Max was infected. He was so sick of catering to that chubby brat. She'd been allowed to slip through the cracks long enough. If he'd had his way, she'd have been in the research lab all along, instead of traipsing around McCarthy infecting other kids.

LOCKED AWAY

It was dark by the time the Suits left. Maxine strained her ears to capture every word that passed between the adults. From what she discerned, her father had thrown his weight around as a representative for the community government.

The Suits weren't intimidated by her father, but Max safely sat in her room until the door slammed on the Suits way out of the house. The adults' conversation did not outright come and say it, but the Suits implied that Max was a problem that would be dealt with now or later. The three compromised, agreeing that when the time came, her parents would take care of the "problem."

Max was still unsure of what this meant.

She stared at the pink walls, at the pictures that had been there as long as she could remember, then closed her eyes. *What would the room look like if I could decorate it any way I want?* she thought. *What would I wear? Who would I be?*

An image of royal purple came to her mind, and she imagined it covering the walls. Polished wood on the floors, a grey and black comforter decorated with silhouettes of birds.

She would have pictures of her nonexistent friends, her parents smiling, and she was pretty sure she wouldn't be wearing skirts and loafers every day to school. Her body would be developed, with round hips and beautiful breasts. Nathan and Ray would fight over courting her.

A knock at the door interrupted the fantasy world Max attempted to create. The lock turned, and the door opened. Max's mother peeked her head in.

"Hey kiddo, we need to talk," she said. She walked over to Max's desk, pulled out the chair and sat down. Her shoulders slumped like a defeated fighter, and she looked at her hands. Her mother had never looked this sad before.

"Max," she said, "your body is going through some changes. There's things that you don't understand and can't control. It's hard to see this happen to you. But we can't let you hurt anyone else." A tear rolled down her Mom's cheek.

"Mom, Nancy dug her fingernails in my arm. Those girls were going to beat me up. What did you want me to do?" Max asked.

"Well, whatever you were going to do to Ms. Texas... Nathan felt compelled to *punch* you to keep you from doing it."

Her mother looked up. Erin's eyes begged for an explanation. Max didn't have one.

"Nathan's a jerk," she said. "He doesn't like me, and he'd use any excuse to hurt me. Even *physically* hurt me. I'm a nobody. A weird freak that makes better grades than everyone else. No matter what I do, people don't like me. I don't care anymore. I'm not getting hurt by these jerks ever again."

Her spine straightened as she thought about defending herself from all the students who thought they could beat her up, whether it was physically, mentally, or emotionally.

Distracted by the conversation downstairs all evening, Max had forgotten about the punch. She touched her cheek, marked by Nathan. Their conversation earlier in the afternoon had made her realize he might be protecting her more than her own parents were.

"I'm going to do my best to be there for you Max," her mother said. "I love you. I've loved you since the first time I held you in my arms. Please always remember that." She pushed herself up from the chair, walked over to Max, and kissed her lightly on the forehead.

Max looked into her Mother's eyes. "Is that all you wanted to say?"

"We'll talk later. Our big priority is to go to commissary tomorrow and spend those vouchers, even if it is for a couple new bras."

Her mother turned away and walked out the door. She didn't close it, which relieved Max; it meant she wasn't locked in for the night. Max walked over and closed the door herself.

She leaned on it as she finally felt the changes of her life seeping in. The burden of a changing body, the conflicts with other students, and the shift in her parents' behavior weighed on her.

Max sunk to the floor. She propped her feet on the back of the door. No one was trying to get in, but she felt like she needed to block the world out.

She smiled, then closed her eyes. She began to imagine her alternate world again. The purple paint was back on the walls, the pictures of dutiful friends resurfaced on her desk.

Just as she started to visualize herself in clothes that accentuated her new body, she was interrupted by a clinking sound at the window. She looked over. For all she knew, it could have been a bug trying to get to the light.

It happened again, but this time she saw the grey rock touch the window. She rolled over, and crawled to investigate. She peeked over the windowsill, squinting to see who'd tossed rocks at her. She saw the blonde wavy hair first—of course:

Nathan.

She shook her head; the boy only knew how to do things violently. He definitely was persistent. She pushed open the window and leaned out.

"What do you want?" She called out to him. "Want to put a bruise on my other cheek?"

Nathan put his finger to his lips. Max mouthed, *What?* He held up his right hand, and Max squinted as he pointed at what appeared to be a white ball with his left hand and made a throwing motion. She nodded, and readied herself for the catch.

The ball sailed past her, into the room and bouncing across the floor, hitting the back wall. She scrambled over to grab it, removing the rubber band that held a crumpled piece of paper in place.

It read, *Max, They are giving you time to see what you will do. Don't trust your parents. They may love you, but they will do what Rothgen wants them to. I want you to be safe. Meet me at school tomorrow at 8 am in the chemistry lab. Be safe, Nathan.*

Max mindlessly placed the paper back around the ball and snapped the rubber band in place. She dropped the ball softly down to Nathan. The glow from the dining room window lit his face as he caught the ball.

He looked up at her and smiled, then darted toward home. The smile on his face had been different this time. It had been soft, sweet, and kind. The kind of smile she had always wanted Nathan to give her.

The door opened behind her. She didn't want to turn around and face these strangers who no longer had her best interests at heart.

"Everything okay in here?" Max's Dad said. "I thought I heard a thump." His voice sounded false and restrained, as it had since she'd pummeled Sue York in the face with the volleyball last week.

He knew exactly what was wrong with her, he knew what Rothgen planned to do with her, and he couldn't be trusted.

"I'm good," she said. "I needed some fresh air. I'm still recovering." She turned around far enough for him to see the side of her face, but not her eyes.

Her father took in a sharp breath. It sounded like someone had punched him in the gut.

"What's wrong?" Max asked. She had not wanted to make eye contact with him, but she wanted to know why that sound had come from him.

"Nothing," he said. "You looked just like your mother when you turned. It surprised me for a moment." His face was pale and sad, and there were tears in his eyes. The false tone was gone.

"Dad, I *never* look like Mom. She has red hair, freckles, and green eyes…" She wanted to continue comparing herself to her mother, but the look on her father's face said she needed to stop.

"We all take a little something from our parents, even if we don't want to." Her father had regained his strange, new political tone. "Sleep tight."

He shut the door. She heard the click of the lock.

They had forgotten that she had not eaten, gone to the bathroom, brushed her teeth, or washed her face.

Something was different now. He wasn't her Dad anymore. He didn't care about her comfort. He cared about keeping her locked in a room he knew she couldn't escape from. Maxine wasn't an idiot, there was no way she could successfully jump out her bedroom window.

Max laid down on the bed in her school clothes and closed her eyes, trying to fight back tears. They rolled down her face anyway. She begged for one of her spells to start so she could black out and not remember this feeling of pure aloneness.

She stayed the same, and remembered every tear.

CHAPTER 10

Nancy Oregon walked through the thick double doors of the Corbin Rothman Medical Center. The stark white walls and bright blue lights of the corridor contrasted with the cold grey day outside. As her eyes adjusted, she saw someone walking toward her. It looked like one of the young medical techs.

At least the trip to the hospital wouldn't be a *total* waste. She could talk to the med techs and learn more about their job. She'd thought it would be something fun to do for a couple of years after high school, before she got married and had a child.

As she drew closer, Nancy frowned. This one wasn't very cute. Sure, she was physically fit, with straight, shiny brown hair, but her skin was dull, and scarred from acne. Nancy hoped when she was twenty she wouldn't have pimples like that.

"Nancy?" the homely tech asked. She held out her hand. "I'm Becca. How are you?"

Nancy stared at Becca's outstretched hand. Her pause was too long. Becca gently took Nancy's bag from her.

"Let's get you settled in your room." Becca turned back toward the long corridor and began walking. Nancy followed.

"Hey!" Mr. Oregon said. "Aren't you going to give me a hug?"

Nancy stopped and turned. "You're not coming with me?"

Mr. Oregon shook his head and opened his arms. Nancy ran to him and pressed her cheek against his chest. His heart raced.

"Daddy, it isn't fair. You should come with me!"

"Ah princess, you're going to the ward specially

made for beautiful little girls like you. No Daddies allowed."

"I love you. Mommy would be so proud," Nancy said as she pushed away. She looked down at the bite on her arm. "This better not leave a scar."

Mr. Oregon grabbed her and pulled her close to him once again. "My baby, you will always be the most beautiful girl in the world."

He pushed her toward the med tech and gave a final nod of approval.

"Let's go," Becca said with a cheerful smile. "I'm going to show you all kinds of interesting parts of the hospital. I'll even show you how to take someone's blood pressure."

Becca stared at Nancy through the two-way mirror. She scrunched her nose in disgust as she watched Nancy pick her nose then proceed to wipe the contents of her finger between the mattress and box springs. A cold hand gripped her shoulder.

"Has she shown any signs of turning?" Dr. Pennsylvania asked.

"No. The only thing she has done is show she's

a little gross and obsessed with her appearance,"
Becca said calmly.

Dr. Pennsylvania made her nervous. His
calculating and flat demeanor unnerved her. She
imagined that at a moment's notice, he would
arbitrarily dissect her as easily as any test subject.

SCIENCE

Sun rays tickled Max's face through thin pink curtains. She loved the way the sunrise looked and felt during autumn. She saw the amber color from behind closed eyelids, but didn't want to open her eyes.

Everything had been a bad dream.

She was ready to go back to school, be the top-ranked student, and live her normal, nobody life.

The feeling of sticky clothes and bad breath were a rude reminder that she'd been locked in her room overnight. Her final motivation to move was the feeling her bladder might explode. She swung her legs over the side of the bed and headed for the door. She prayed silently that her parents had unlocked it.

The knob gave as she turned it, allowing her the opportunity to escape.

She made a mental note to try to figure out the lock when no one was looking. Being trapped in her room felt smothering. Plus, it meant that they could do what they wished with her.

She headed toward the bathroom. Her mother was cooking, and her father talked in a low voice. From the tone of her mother's voice, she wasn't happy. He must be agreeing with the Suit's plan for getting rid of Max.

Maybe her mother wasn't against her? She hadn't locked the door when she'd left Max's room. Her father had. It didn't matter. As much as Nathan had been crappy to her, he had been more honest than the adults. It surprised her, though; she'd really thought Ray would be the one coming to her rescue.

Max opened the medicine cabinet and grabbed her toothbrush, plastering on some paste and

KATIE CORD

scrubbing vigorously while she continued to think about Ray.

Was he working with Nathan? He definitely seemed anti-Rothgen, but he was the son of Dr. Pennsylvania. Dr. Penn gave her the creeps. He'd lied about not having a daughter, and for whatever reason had compelled Ray to do the same. Ray definitely didn't look like Ellen, but Max didn't look like her parents, either. She remembered he'd left school yesterday morning after talking with Nathan. What was he doing at school if he wasn't planning to student-teach?

Max washed off her toothbrush and shut the cabinet door. It wasn't until she looked in the mirror with washcloth in hand that she saw it: her hair had grown four inches overnight, and her face looked different. She finally looked like a sixteen-year-old, not the chubby twelve-year-old she'd looked like for years.

She touched her face, feeling her sculpted cheekbones, and her new silky, long hair. The new hair held a shine that her dull black hair had never had. She smiled at the new face, held her shoulders

175

back and preened at the lifted chest. Then she went back to her room. She had to meet Nathan in twenty minutes.

Max slipped into her standard grey wool skirt, but it felt like it would fall off if she moved. Her sweater swallowed her whole. She pulled on her stretched-out knee socks, slid into her loafers and headed out of her bedroom.

Before she could make it down the hallway, she had to return to her room. Her skirt was falling down, and her socks had slid to her ankles.

She'd always cursed her mother for keeping a "regular"-sized uniform to give her motivation to lose weight. Today, she yanked it out of the back of the closet and quickly tossed it on. She grabbed her special occasion socks, because she knew they'd fit. She avoided her mirror, as much as she wanted to inspect herself and, she hated to admit it, admire her new look. She had a mission.

As she headed for the door, she heard her mother call for her from the kitchen.

"Max, are you going to have breakfast?" her mother asked. She walked down the hallway toward Max. Then she stopped. Max watched her mother's face. It was filled with confusion, fear, and amazement.

"No thanks. I'm okay," Max said.

"Honey, we have to go to the commissary tonight. There's no way around it." Her mother came forward, hugged her tightly, and kissed her cheek. "Please, please try to stay out of trouble today. I love you, little girl."

Max blushed. She still loved her mother. This woman had helped her in so many ways. It was hard to imagine that she would side with Rothgen to hurt her.

"I gotta go, Mom. I love you too." Max pulled gently away from her mother.

She closed the door behind her. She stepped out onto her doorstep and inhaled the cool crisp air. She started walking toward the high school. She noticed the silver car parked six houses ahead of her. She continued to walk, pretending that she was oblivious to the vehicle and the man inside. Her meeting with Nathan was the priority.

She had gone to school with the same people her

whole life and always been the odd one, bigger on the outside but weaker on the inside. Now it seemed like every second since her birthday, the molecules that made up her being changed.

The school entrance was just ahead. She hoped the Suit didn't try to take her before she could make it in. He'd promised her father that he could take care of the situation. Max was still frustrated at not knowing what *the situation* meant, but Nathan had answers, and she had to get to him.

She reached the steps and breathed a sigh of relief. The Suit had not snagged her this time. Mr. Dakotas stood at the entrance, waving the wand he used every morning at another student. The line was short at eight in the morning. He looked up at Max and paused. He looked nervous as she walked up for her turn.

"Hello, Maxine. Are you ready for the day?" he asked. His voice trembled a little. Max stood taller and smiled confidently.

"I'm ready as I will ever be." She slid her foot out to make her ankle bracelet easily accessible. Mr. Dakotas' hand held a fine tremor as he slowly moved the wand over her ankle. He looked at the reading.

"I need to swipe it one more time. Do you mind?" he asked. This time he swiped quickly, then looked at the new reading. "Okay." He paused. "You can go in." He backed away from her as she entered the large scanner at the door. She heard a thump, and turned to look.

Mr. Dakotas sat in a chair, looking pale and shaky. It scared *her* to see a full-grown adult worried that she would hurt him. She didn't know what she was capable of doing. She just knew that her body was changing fast.

As Max approached the chemistry door, she found Nathan deep in thought reading his textbook, forehead scrunched. She knocked lightly, trying not to scare him. He looked up. At first he appeared taken aback; his eyes widened, then squinted with worry.

"It's happening faster than it happened to her." He frowned. He gently closed his book and placed it in his bag. Then he turned away from her, walking toward the ventilation fans. He flipped the switch on and mumbled. Max could barely make out the words, but she thought he said, "Beautiful."

She blushed. Was he talking about her? Did he think she looked beautiful now that her body was changing?

"Let's go." He headed toward the supply closet.

The room was dark, and though all the bottles were sealed, there was an undeniable smell of elements and compounds brewing on the shelves. Max stepped in first, and Nathan followed. He closed the door behind them and locked it. He dropped his bag on the floor and leaned on the table that held goggles and the logbook. He stared through a bottle of hydrochloric acid as though he could burst it through sheer will.

"This is hard for me to admit and to talk about, but I just need to get it out there," he said.

She stared silently, waiting for what he had to say.

"I've been watching you for a long time." He let out a breath of relief like he'd just admitted a sin.

"That's it?" she asked.

He sighed. "No, that's not it." He ran his fingers

through his blonde hair. She saw in his eyes that he was trying to formulate his words carefully.

"Okay, I got it. You're like my big sister Melissa. She was so smart. Beautiful. I loved her so much. She taught me how to read before I went to school. She encouraged me to play sports even though there was nothing to gain from it. But one day, she blacked out. She wasn't herself. Dr. Penn told my Dad it was seizures. She would be fine. A week or two later, she woke up and looked like a different person. She didn't look like a little girl anymore. She looked like, uh... she looked like you." Nathan pointed up and down at her body before looking away.

"What's wrong with growing up?" Max crossed her arms over her budding breasts.

"The problem is..." He couldn't make himself say it. "The problem is that a week after she started looking like you do now, she killed the mailman, Mr. Kentucky. She opened the door as he was putting the mail in the slot, grabbed him, and ripped his throat out with her teeth."

Max didn't understand what he was saying.

"What does this have to do with me?"

"You're like her," he said again. "She put the body in the basement. Went up to the bathroom, showered, and woke up a day later remembering nothing. My Dad found the body and called the Suits. He thought someone else had done it. They retrieved the body and then it was silent until the next day, when the new mailman shot her."

Nathan walked toward her. "You're going to kill someone. You already bit Nancy. Once someone is bitten, it will heal, but then eventually the disease will take over their body, and then it is over for them. The war will start over again. All of our parents sacrificing their freedom will have done it for nothing."

"I'm not going to kill anyone," Max said, shaking her head in disbelief. "Stop talking like this. Your sister had a mental problem. She's probably in some area of the medical center where they can watch her all the time. And Nancy, there's nothing wrong with her that a little antibiotic ointment won't treat."

"It gets worse. You're going to need to eat

human flesh to continue to grow and maintain the way you are. If you don't you'll revert back."

Max couldn't register any of what he was saying, except that he'd called her beautiful.

"What's wrong with me, then?" she questioned. "Isn't there a way to fix me?" It was better for her to start thinking about facts and information than feelings.

"Max, I'm a hundred percent sure that Erin Massachusetts is not your Mom," Nathan said. He grabbed her elbows, seemingly anticipating that this would take her over the edge. She shook off his hands.

"How can you talk like that?"

"Max, you've got the type of zombie virus that only happens to people who are born with it. If Erin were your real Mom, she would have been killed during the war. I don't know if your Dad is your real Dad or not, but Erin can't be your Mom."

"Why do you think this is happening now?"

"From what my Dad has told me, the disease starts to convert around puberty. That's what happened to my sister."

"Was Ellen Penn like me?"

"Not that I know of."

"Oh, but Ray Penn is... I just know it. I could sense it. There was just a feeling of *knowing* between us."

"Ray bit Ellen when they were little kids. It took twelve years for the virus to break her down. She looked healthy the whole time. Their Dad killed her at home when she went all zombie on him."

"Why aren't you worried about Ray?" she asked. "Why aren't you helping him?"

"Dr. Penn is giving Ray flesh," Nathan said, with disgust in his voice.

"Oh." Max was silent. If what Nathan said was true, why did Ray look so pale and thin? "He still looks like I did before this transition, just bigger."

"The flesh is already dead. If you want to keep the body, you have to eat from living people."

"How do you know all of this?"

"My Dad. He's a truck driver," Nathan said, moving half a step closer. "He drives to all the communities. He trades information. There are *loads* of kids like you. Some of the other communities sent them out on their own before the Suits could kill them. Others wait until they kill someone. Our community is the most discreet."

Nathan was right in front of Max. She felt his warmth next to her. It made her breathe faster. The warning bell rang that school would be starting shortly. Max jumped, brushing against Nathan, and he braced her.

"Be careful," he said. "We're in a room full of volatile chemicals."

Max wasn't worried about the volatile chemicals, but the strange stirrings inside of her. She finally felt courageous enough to take what she wanted, and what she wanted was for Nathan to kiss her. She leaned forward, into him. Her newly-formed breasts responded to the pressure of his body next to hers. He took a deep breath.

"Max, I've always liked you," he said. "Your intelligence, your smile. But nothing can happen between us. It's my duty to help you so you don't end up a slave to flesh like Ray, or dead like Ellen and my sister. I can't do this."

He backed away from her, grabbed his

backpack, and headed into the classroom. He left Max standing in the dark, wondering what had just happened.

She followed Nathan into the bright light.

She and Nathan had forgotten there was a class that utilized the chemistry room for homeroom. Twenty-six seniors all turned to stare at Max as she walked briskly behind Nathan on their way out of the room. A male voice from the back of the room said, "Is that Mess-a-shit-etts? What happened to her?"

Max held her head up high and walked out of the room. She felt rejected by Nathan, but she accepted his reasons for not kissing her. He cared. She knew now that he felt it was important to save her life. She couldn't believe that Ray was a flesh-eater. It made her question what else he was up to.

"Hey, I'll see you later today," Nathan said. "Try to stay out of trouble. I've got more to tell you. We've got to get a plan in place. Time is running out." He squeezed her hand and gently smiled at her.

Max walked to her homeroom, torn between

rejection, acceptance, and the quiet rejoicing of an acknowledged crush. She was almost at the door when she noticed Ray Pennsylvania at the end of the hallway, waving at her.

He smiled when she saw him, and beckoned her forth. She felt drawn to him. There was a synergy there between them; an unspoken community that she didn't totally understand.

"Hey, I haven't seen you all week." He smiled. After her growth spurt, she reached the tip of Ray's nose.

"What's up, Ray?" she asked. "Are you even really student-teaching here?" She didn't want to give away her feeling of comfort at being in his presence.

"Okay, you got me," he said. "I don't teach here. I was sent here to be a special present for you." His smile was cocky as he relaxed against the corner of the hallway, placing his hands in the pockets of his khakis. He looked her up and down. "I knew you were going to be beautiful once it kicked in," he said.

"What do you mean? I'm the same person I've
187

always been."

Ray closed his eyes, leaned his head against the wall, and gently rocked back and forth.

"Let's be real: you were a fat, homely girl who couldn't get anything but negative attention, even with your stellar grades. Do you plan on trying to keep it, or will you take the compromise and the plan my father is going to offer you?" he asked.

"You mean eat dead flesh, like you?" she offered back.

"I figured the blonde wonder would try to get to you first," Ray said. "You know he's trying to *save* you, right?" Ray stood up straight. "There's nothing to save. We're a new race. You got a couple options, and I don't think you're going to like either of them, but if you don't choose, the virus and your body will choose for you."

"I'm not going to kill anyone. I'm not eating flesh. I'll figure something out. So what if Nathan wants to help me? What's it to you?"

Maxine tried to turn away from him, but Ray grabbed her arm.

"Look," he said, "I gave my sister a death

sentence when she was two years old. I didn't even know it. Do you think you can keep from hurting people? You can't. *Nathan* can't even do this for you."

Ray pulled her in, placing his mouth hard on hers. He grabbed her breast, squeezing tightly as he parted her lips with his tongue. Part of her wanted to pursue the feeling. It was the part that was like him. The old Max pushed him away. This was not how she wanted her first kiss to be.

"I don't believe you," Max said, wiping her mouth. Ray's magnetism must have all been the modified virus in their bodies, trying to mate them.

He grinned mischievously, then laughed. This laugh was maniacal and full of anger.

"It's okay, Max. I didn't take anything away from you. You won't ever be able to kiss Nathan. All you need to do is get enough body fluid in there or break his skin and he's a goner. They don't turn like us. They look like the creepy biters from the war."

Max walked away, blocking out his venomous words. He continued to ramble on about their kind.

She headed toward her homeroom. She was late. It would add to her detention time. It didn't really bother her. In her gut, she was pretty sure she wouldn't make it to her second detention, let alone any added on.

Ms. Maine was a sweet teacher who had never said a discouraging word to Max, but as soon as Max entered homeroom, she looked her up and down. "Maxine," she said, "you need to go to the principal's office. You've been reported for breaking dress code. I see why, now."

Ms. Maine looked at the grey skirt that grazed above Max's knees. A line of disapproval spread across her forehead.

Max rolled her eyes and threw her hands up in the air. Mike Carolina whistled as Max turned around to leave the room. She waved her hand back toward the classroom, shooing his appreciation back from whence it came.

As far as she was concerned, Mike Carolina could sit in the back of the room and *eat* the fingers he'd used to whistle at her. She was still the loser she had always been; now, she was a loser in a snug sweater and a shorter skirt.

"So, you're becoming the bad girl of the school, huh?" Ray said, stepping out from behind the classroom door.

"I thought you got the hint. I'm not interested in anything that either you or your father have to offer me. I'm not eating flesh. Dead, alive, it doesn't matter. I'll die first. Okay? *Do you hear me?*"

She headed straight for Mr. Oregon's office. Ray walked close to her, bumping her hip as they walked. Her loafers echoed through the quiet hallway with each angry step.

"You're not listening to me," Ray insisted. "You don't have a choice. It's going to happen. Why not do it on your own terms? I can take you to the hospital right now. We can get it over with in a nice, controlled environment.

"I met you last week to get this set up. With your intelligence, the Rothman family has personally decided to keep you. Max, you could have power, and now you're hot as hell. Honestly, I didn't look that much different, so I never felt the need to kill. I'd kill to touch your bod—"

MAXINE

Ray stopped talking abruptly.

Distracted by the ideas of murder, corporate families that owned the world, and how to keep Ray from touching her body, Max looked up. In front of Mr. Oregon's office stood her father and the Suit who had stalked her for the last two weeks.

Ray slipped his hand around her upper arm and started guiding her toward the men.

"Well, it looks like they couldn't wait to let me finish my job," he mumbled.

CHAPTER 11

Justin Texas squinted down the hallway. From what he could discern, the scraggly, pale-faced punk was dragging the Massachusetts girl down the hall. She'd turned into a true beauty just like they said, but nobody was fooling him. That girl needed a bullet in the head. He could pop them both right now, if he was ready for Rothgen to put him down as well.

"Do you think you can handle this?" Justin said.

Rob nodded.

"Are you sure?" Justin looked down at the syringe Rob held. The man was weaving it back and forth between his fingers. Justin felt the need to point out the obvious. "You know, if you inject yourself, you ain't going to be any good to any of us."

"Oh," Rob mumbled. He looked down at the floor in shame.

"It's all right. This is a tough situation." Justin paused, trying to think of what to say. He figured something was better than nothing. "It's the right thing to do. If you hadn't signed on here, she'd be dead already."

Rob gave Justin a sideways glance, then said, "Just keep her held down, I'll get this done."

"Not a problem." Justin cracked his knuckles. "If I can't stop a sixteen-year-old girl, then what good am I?"

"Daddy?" the girl said as the punk dragged her closer.

Her expression reminded Justin of the women picking their husbands up from the precinct after they'd been caught propositioning hookers. Without thinking, his hand went to his gun holster. He knew she could pop off into her un-human version at any time.

"Maxine, I need you to listen to—" Rob faltered as her face went from alabaster to a blue-toned white. Her shoulders scrunched and her pupils dilated to the point where her eyes looked like two lumps of coal.

She pulled away from the punk and lunged toward her father. Swiftly, the syringe plunged into her neck, and without pausing, her Dad injected her with its contents. The girl fell to the floor.

Rob leaned down to check on her. Then he looked up at Justin Texas. "What will you do if you can't stop a sixteen-year-old girl?"

LAB RAT

"How's she doing?"

Voices bounced back and forth through Max's head. Her eyelids felt heavy, and she didn't think she could open them. She wasn't sure how long she had been this way. The last thing she remembered was Ray pinching her arm as he handed her over to a Suit.

This Suit had looked as though Rothgen had genetically engineered him to be the supreme super-creep agent. She remembered his pores were so big she'd thought you could stick a pencil in one of them. He'd had rough hands for someone who drove a car and sat around stalking people. Then the sting had happened. What was the sting?

Oh yeah, she thought, *my freaking* father *shot me up with some drug so I'd pass out.*

There had been no remorse in her father's face. No look of helplessness or sorrow. If she remembered correctly, she'd seen his tongue sticking slightly out to the side, as though he were trying extra hard to inject her.

Maybe she had made it up. The Suit might have had a gunman sitting at her house, pointed on her Mom. She wouldn't blame her Dad for choosing her Mom over her. They'd made a pact to live the rest of their lives together.

She felt a dull sensation. It was slight, and she couldn't really figure out what was wrong. Then she heard the voices again. She cleared her mind, focusing on them individually.

"She can't feel it. Just get it over with." The voice leaned in. "Here, let me roll her over."

The dull sensation was her captors moving her.

She breathed quietly as she listened, to count the voices. There were two for sure, but it seemed like the two were reporting to someone else in the room.

"Its heart rate remains at approximately thirty-five to forty regardless of the stimuli. Epinephrine up to 1000 milligrams does not increase the rate. Sedation works, but only in large volumes. The propofol is keeping it sedated, but we're unsure how long that will work. We've been re-dosing every twelve to fifteen minutes. It currently appears to be out. What else would you like us to do?"

The person's voice reminded her of the time she'd dissected a frog and recited the anatomy to her biology teacher. Except now, *she* was the frog.

"Okay, that's fine. No problem."

The person must be talking into a headset. She couldn't hear what the unknown person was instructing him to do, but her arms began to sear with pain. *There must have been a struggle*, she thought. Why else would her arms feel like someone had squeezed her in so many places?

"So, he said leave it. They want to see what happens when it wakes up."

"So they want it awake?" the other voice questioned, soft. She couldn't tell if it was female or male.

"Yeah, Dr. Penn's freak is going to try to talk to it again. Seems they want it to cooperate. Between it and Dr. Penn's mongrel, they want to start on the new phase of Rothgen's plan."

In Max's mind, the one doing all the talking looked like her history teacher, Mr. Idaho, except with slimy black hair that he probably combed straight back, and a white lab coat bursting at the seams.

"Let's just get out of here before it wakes up. I can't stand to look at it when it's in the other form." Max imagined the soft-voiced person shuddering at the thought of her angry side.

She didn't even know what that side looked like. She knew what it felt like right before it came over her, but nothing during. Was she that grotesque?

The people watching her had called Ray a mongrel, and they'd referred to her as an "it." The two were performing a job, and they didn't think of her as a human now. She guessed she *wasn't* fully human. That might be why she was so attracted to Ray. Maybe they really were the same.

A whooshing sound interrupted her thoughts as cool air blew over her. She heard one of them say, "Dr. Penn, she's ready for you." Then the air was pulled back with the sound of the door closing.

"Max, you can quit pretending you're unconscious. They're gone," Ray said.

Max continued to lay still. She wasn't sure she could open her eyes, and had not dared try while the other two had been in the room.

"Look, I can come over there and help you wake up or you can just open your damn eyes," Ray said.

Max lay still. Ray moved closer. There had to be a pheromone triggered by the virus that allowed her to know her own. Ray touched her arm. His hands were ice cold.

No one had ever told her that she was this cold. Of course, she tried not to touch people.

His fingers dug into her arm. It felt like he was stabbing her with needles.

She opened her eyes and looked at him.

His smile appeared harmless, but when she

looked into his eyes, they were cold and clinical.

"Are you the Dr. Penn they're talking about? You can't be more than twenty. How's that possible?" Max asked. She swallowed hard, trying to remain calm.

"I was pulled out of school at nine, and sent here to the medical facility to start training," he said. "Of course I missed the idea of being normal, but what's normal?"

She looked down to see a large needle near her wrist. It looked like he planned to torture her by stimulating her nerves until she begged for mercy.

He pulled back the needle and placed it on a metal tray. Then he turned back to her. "You know, if you'd been a boy, they would have done the same for you. You actually scored higher than me on all the aptitude tests. But Rothgen doesn't want any women in power in their new world. Gets too complicated when you little lovelies can do what you want."

Max wasn't sure whether Ray was trying to bring out her other side or he was just being a jerk.

"That's fine, Ray. I'm glad I wasn't brought to

this place and made to eat people. I was allowed to be a kid. And, you know, eat *real* food like a *real* person."

"I wasn't *made* to do *anything*. I was told what would happen to me if I didn't. It wasn't my fault. I rationalized my options and started eating the flesh way before puberty. I've never had one of those nasty spells like the rest of you. I'm *lucky*." Ray smiled smugly.

"You started eating it before you had to?" Max gasped. She couldn't imagine eating someone. Her stomach clenched at the thought.

"Yes, that's why I matured a little easier than you. Of course, poor Ellen was completely normal until the virus switched on..." Ray looked over Max and stared at the facing wall.

"You know, if my father didn't think his little girl might be special. We might have been able to do something, but no, he didn't want her to be a lab rat. He already knew they just don't change like us. Their bodies react exactly like they did when the original virus occurred, except it takes longer and they can't nail down every mutation. Of course, once they become full blown zombies, the only option is a bullet to the head... *or* hack them to pieces, but that gets a little messy."

Max wanted to get up from table and smack Ray in the face until he made sense, but the leather straps around her arms and legs kept her secure.

He justified his behavior with science. She wanted him to act like their humanity mattered, say they were alive, that she had a choice on whether she ate or not.

"So, do you know what happened to your mother?" she asked.

"Same thing that happened to pretty much *all* the mothers of the kids who've got this problem. She was stupid and contracted the virus. She's dead. My father replaced her. Just like your Mom and Dad. Well, except neither of your parents is your biological parent. They admitted it when they came into the community," Ray said.

Tears welled in the corners of Max's eyes. She didn't want to think about them.

"Yeah, according to the records, Erin Massachusetts cut you out of a lady as she lay dying. That's pretty messed up," Ray said as he toyed with a sharp-looking saw.

Max realized she needed to get up from the table, regardless of what Ray planned to do to her.

"So, what's the game plan? Those two before said you were coming in here to convince me to be part of the Rothgen plan. The plan is? I'm guessing I don't get to refuse, regardless of what you tell me. Let's just get it over with, then. I'm ready. I just want to be up off this table when it happens."

"It's like this," he said. "You're going to start eating flesh. You'll kill a few people and keep looking incredibly hot, and then we're going to see if we can make a couple of babies. Those babies are what Rothgen is most interested in."

Ray smiled a crooked smile. His breathing became excited. "The choice for you is whether you want to try the natural way or do this the sterile, clinical way..."

Max saw the telephone light blinking on and off. There was no ring. Ray squinted as he watched it flicker, too.

"Damn it," he mumbled, walking over to pick

up the phone. He grabbed the receiver and spoke in a low voice. He was on for several minutes before Max heard a slam. The door swished open quickly, and Ray walked out without looking at Max. His face was scrunched up like that of a child who'd received a scolding.

As he walked out the door, a familiar face appeared. It was Gretchen from physical inspections. Her smile radiated across the room. She walked directly toward Max and removed the leather straps from her ankles.

CHAPTER 12

"Well, personally, I think she is a sweetie, but a little too smart if you know what I mean," Gretchen said as she filed her nails.

"Still jealous. This Nancy girl is killing me. I wish she'd just convert already, or *something*. Staring at her all day is sooo painful."

Becca dramatically rolled over on her back, threw her arm over her eyes, and groaned. "I don't know how you can just stare at yourself all day. She doesn't read, she just stares, and primps. Kind of makes me wonder what the hell she was doing with her time before she ended up in the facility."

MAXINE

Gretchen looked over at Becca lying on her thin plastic mattress. She knew why Dr. Penn didn't give her Maxine to work with. The girl was dramatic, couldn't handle even a simple task like observing someone for conversion.

Gretchen had monitored a group of thirty-six including Maxine for a year before things had gotten even remotely exciting. Becca was not pretty either—not like her, at least.

It was part of the plan she guessed: make a shy little fatty feel like one of the pretty girls, and then maybe she'd eat flesh. Hopefully the plan would work, because she couldn't think of any other one unless she put Maxine in a room with a gun to her head and *made* the girl eat someone.

"Ha. Try working with a know-it-all that thinks she's too good to be the creator of a new race. That is *painful*. I've got this one chance to show them what I'm made of. I want an exceptional husband, and I seriously want to live in the City Upon the Hill."

Gretchen put her nail file in her nightstand and laid her head on her pillow. "I can't live in this hovel too much longer," she said, casting her arms around the dull grey walls of the room. Their matching wool blankets only magnified the dreariness.

"So, what do you plan to do?"

"Whatever it takes," Gretchen mumbled, and closed her eyes.

EXPLANATION OR EXCUSES

"Hey Maxine, how are you? I think these guys are doing this all wrong. How do they expect you to feel like you're part of the process if they treat you like a problem?" Gretchen smiled reassuringly at Max as she removed the wrist restraints. She looked Max up and down. "They said you would be absolutely beautiful once you transitioned, but I didn't believe it. You were so flabby and pale. The others that have come through have nothing on you."

Maxine blushed. This was a beautiful young woman who had seen Maxine down to her underpants many times. She'd seemed honest and forthright with Max every time she'd worked with Dr. Penn, but Max was aware Gretchen was a pawn just like everyone else.

"How many have come through?" Max asked as she rubbed her wrist, trying to bring back the circulation.

"You all are a special group. There aren't that many of you, but enough that Rothgen wants to study you. It won't hurt, I promise. You don't have to sleep with Ray, but they will want you to try to have a baby once you start eating."

Gretchen was sweet and kind. She said things as though they would happen. Max had always liked her, but the woman discreetly bossing Max around was no better than Ray doing it in the open.

"What if I don't want to eat?" Max challenged, delicately sitting up on the side of the metal gurney.

"Do you seriously want to go back to being ugly?" Gretchen looked in a hand mirror. She was perfect: her height, her weight, the way her hair fell onto her shoulders in waves. "I couldn't do it. I'll be honest with you. Take a look." She handed Max the mirror.

Max grabbed it from her and stared at herself. Her large black eyes were amplified by high cheekbones and pink, pouty lips. Her black hair was shiny, and her skin looked flawless. She would intimidate even Esther Hampshire with these looks.

Her breasts now stood out on her chest, and it felt like her hips bones had widened. She wished for one second that she could be back in that locker room, showing all of this off. Pointing out the flaws of the girls who had made her feel like a freak.

"If someone told me that I could be beautiful forever, never age, and look like you if I ate uncooked meat, I'd do it," Gretchen said with sincerity.

"It's not meat. It's people," Max mumbled.

"We wouldn't feed you anyone who was a decent person," Gretchen assured her.

"Can I be alone to think about all this?" Max said. The idea of justifying cannibalism by eating bad people didn't sit well with her.

"Sure. I was going to take you to your new room anyway."

Gretchen handed her a pair of slippers. She appeared so caring and kind, but Max wasn't stupid. They wanted results. Ray and his Dad were probably going to receive accolades if they could breed some perfect monster from her genes. The tech would probably be offered a better marriage proposal if she could show how resourceful she was. Everyone would win... except Max.

Max slipped the cool cotton slippers on. Her hospital gown was a thick rough material that covered her down to her mid-calves. The room was cold. She crossed her arms, getting used to the responses of her body. Her new long, thick hair irritated her.

She'd watched the glowing girls flip their thick, lush hair back and forth and been envious. It had never occurred to her that it could be a pain.

She stood up and followed Gretchen. Max was about two inches taller than her now. She could probably take her, but that would just lead to more sedation, which definitely was not what she wanted.

The pair walked out of the sliding doors into a

grey hallway that was dimly lit. There were windows on each side, with bright white rooms like the one Max had been in. Looking inside the rooms, Max saw young people in various stages of consciousness.

It wasn't until they were at the end of the hallway that she saw something that frightened her.

A girl about her age was leaned over an older male. The man looked to be in his thirties—well, what was left of him looked to be in his thirties. The young woman chewed at his torso. Her skin was ashen, her hair was dark and curly, and her eyes were glazed over with some kind of film. Satisfaction crossed over her lips as flesh and blood dripped from them. She looked up at the window as though she could sense Max staring at her.

"She can't see us, but the virus inside of you can sense others, and it sends a message to your cells to respond. If too many of you are in one place, you can become like a pack," Gretchen said matter-of-factly, then started walking.

"Let's go. You're going to love your new room. It's been specifically designed from your personal preferences." She talked excitedly and in a high, girly voice, as though they were best friends.

Max knew better. She didn't want to be that girl in the room, eating someone else. Had the girl made the choice to feed, or had they forced her? Even if they had, when the other side of her kind came out, it looked like they just went for flesh naturally.

Maybe that was what Ray was trying to tell her? He could've made the choice to feed before he turned to keep himself from becoming like that girl. Max didn't want to sympathize with him. He was part of the team that had captured her.

"So, have you tried to breed any of the rest of those people?" Max asked.

"Max, we've been collecting blood samples and DNA since we realized there was a hybrid of the disease. The problem is that most parents won't report it, if their kid could be infected. Your father reported you when they signed the agreement to live in the community. We've been analyzing changes in your DNA since you were two."

Gretchen led her through a set of double doors

and into bright, rushing light. They were in a different part of the medical center. Max turned around to see if the department they'd come from was labeled.

The sign above the double doors read: Morgue.

Gretchen bounced down the hall more than she walked. She delighted in helping others, it was clear, but how much did she delight in the science behind it all, no matter the cost to the subject?

The two walked further down the hallway until they reached a room with a sign beside the door that read, *Massachusetts, M.* Below it read, *High Security Limited Access.* Gretchen opened the door, and Max walked into a room that was similar to one from her dreams.

The walls were a slate grey with white trim. A fluffy purple comforter with an arrangement of soft pillows were arranged on the bed, and facing a large window was a desk for her to write at. Max went to the window. Below, she saw the woods that led out past the community. Max walked over and sat on the edge of the bed.

"So, you and Ray have been selected to breed

217

after you feed. There is a group of doctors here who can take your eggs and put them with Ray's sperm, then put it back in your body. They used to do it all the time with healthy humans, before the war. The important thing is the fetus has to gestate in your tummy. The filtration of the baby's little sac called the placenta will regulate your blood and the virus through to the fetus."

Gretchen rambled on about the process of pregnancy and fetal development. The more she went on, the more her voice sounded childish.

Max laid down on the bed and closed her eyes. "You know my Mom was a nurse before the war. She told me about the female reproductive system. She didn't patronize me either."

Silence.

After a long, uncomfortable pause, Gretchen said, "I think this has all overwhelmed you. I'm going to let you rest. Then we'll talk some more. I think you are taking this very well, and everything is going to be okay."

She carefully backed out of the room, watching Max's every move. As she closed the door, Max

heard a sound that was becoming all too familiar:
the click of a lock.

Not ready to be a wife?

Sign up for med tech training at Corben Rothman Hospital.

We can always use a smart, obedient girl like you!

CHAPTER 13

Erin and Rob Massachusetts sat in their quiet, semi-dark living room, staring at the amber glow from their fireplace.

"What do you miss the most?" Rob asked.

Erin placed her hand in Rob's and squeezed. "Does it matter?"

"Yeah, I think it does," Rob said as he pulled his hand away. He turned to her. "I miss doing whatever the hell I want. I miss Boston and being anonymous. I have so many regrets and wishes. I wish I wouldn't have been a coward. I wish I'd lived dangerously at least once. I was a boring freaking lawyer, too afraid to even yell at a guy for harassing an old lady on the train."

Erin didn't look at Rob. Instead she stared at the fire. They sat in silence. The ticking clock on the mantle was the only sound in the room. This went on for a while before a large log they'd placed on the fire split in half and made a sharp crack. It was a loud enough sound to break Erin's trance.

"I miss my husband, my baby who never made it out of me alive, and most of all, I miss my dignity," she said, tears rolling down her face.

Rob tried to reassure her. "You had no choice in any of those things."

"Really? All I can think of is how we could have hidden. We could have taken Maxine out to Purgatory, taught her to control the biters ourselves," Erin said.

A wave of relief hit her as she revealed her guilt. The feeling flooded her, and she couldn't stop. "We let that baby down, we let that girl we raised down. We promised to take care of her. We handed her to them on a silver platter. There is nothing left for us here. What good are we to Rothgen?"

A knock on the door silenced her.

Erin's eyes widened. Rob gave her a questioning look. The knock came again. Erin wiped her eyes. Rob stood up, straightened his shirt, and walked to the door. Erin stayed on the couch, facing the fireplace. She didn't move. She gripped the couch cushions, her stomach in knots.

Then, it happened: the sound of firecrackers popping. She closed her eyes. He hadn't even fought them. There wasn't any fight left in either of them, really.

In her mind, she imagined herself darting over to the lamp and tossing it at him. She knew it was a him. They wouldn't let a female be an assassin.

The door creaked. The footsteps neared.

Erin stood up and turned to face her death. They had sent a mailman. He looked through her. She expected as much. It wasn't personal. She heard the pop, and felt the bullet sear through her. She held herself up. There were two more pops, and more pain. Now, she had to force herself to stay upright.

The impact of third bullet knocked Erin backward, breaking the coffee table.

MAXINE

She heard the mailman coming toward her. She looked up to see him inspecting her. As much as she wanted to play dead, her body demanded she fight to continue breathing. Blood rolled from her mouth and nose and there wasn't a damn thing she could do but try not to strangle.

She saw his face. Middle-aged just like her, except there was an arrogance and element of vacant sociopath that she'd only seen on her worst days back in the emergency room. He spit on her then put the gun to her head.

The last thing she heard was, "What a bitter little bitch, wouldn't even lay down at the end."

PREPARATION

There was no calendar or clock in the room. Max started marking the days down in her journal. She was surprised they hadn't given her the means to track the length of her captivity.

It seemed like she had been in the facility for weeks, but she knew it had only been six days. In that span, they had pulled her out of the room seventeen times.

The first couple of times, they'd rushed in the room, held her down, and shot her with a tranquilizer gun. After a while, as soon as she heard the lock click, she held her arms out in a sign of surrender and let them inject her with the syringe.

Even though she'd never fought them, her body was battered and bruised from the testing alone. *Besides,* she thought. *If I want to see evidence of the experiments they are performing on me, I have to cooperate.*

She'd awakened during one procedure to find a wand rubbing over her lower abdomen while a large syringe with an even longer needle withdrew what she assumed were eggs. They'd immediately sedated her again.

Before she fell asleep, she heard a valuable piece of information: one of the doctors complained that no drugs worked on her the same way twice. Her body adapted quickly to change; it was one of the miracles of the virus.

Max knew she wasn't ready to be a mother, whether the children would know her or not. She deserved the right to choose the destiny of her genetics without Rothgen or their doctors playing mad scientist.

She really wished someone could save her. She figured it would have to be herself. Her own parents had sold her out. She wasn't sure of the price, but she hoped it was for a good reason.

Maxine walked over to the mirror and looked at herself. The fine little black mustache was gone, her eyebrows arched perfectly, her eyes held life that hadn't been there before, and below the neck, her breasts and hips were those of a woman.

Every day, a new attractive guy brought her meals and tried to strike up a conversation. They all bragged about being medical students, and appeared to be well-read and highly intelligent, but they were older, and it intimidated her, regardless of how pretty they said she was.

They talked to her like she was a woman, like someone even older than sixteen, but inside, she still felt like a little girl.

Ray forcing his lips on her didn't count. She was glad he was gone. There was a connection between them that she couldn't stop. The magnetism of their bodies trying to replicate the virus frightened her. She'd been so charmed by him at first she'd never questioned him. But now she was certain it wasn't because she liked what he had to say or who he was.

She sat at her desk and looked past the forest that shielded the community. What was out beyond it? The videos showed the world as a harsh and savage place that wasn't safe to live in. All of those rescued were worth saving, according to the Rothgen rhetoric, but were there humans still living outside of the walls?

Regardless, Rothgen would not release a highly prized possession like her without a fight.

From three stories up, she watched large trucks back up to the docking area and as unmarked boxes were carried off by strangers. She was sure the items in those boxes were furthering Dr. Penn and Rothgen's agenda.

She shuddered. The doctor had to be soulless; he'd killed Ellen and pretended like she hadn't existed.

Daughter, she thought. She had been one of those. Then her parents had given her over to be a test subject and breeder of the new race of infected people. The idea of pale thin children who could live forever as long as they ate flesh turned her stomach. She didn't want to kill herself, but why would she want to create more flesh eaters?

Someone knocked on the door. She didn't expect them to ask permission to enter; they never did. The lock clicked over and the door opened. Max just stared out the window. There was no use turning around to protest.

"Maaaaaax. How are you doing in here?" Gretchen asked sweetly.

"I'm as good as any half-dead girl can be. How about yourself?" Max's voice held no emotion. She stared out the window. Behind her, she heard the rustling of plastic.

"Well, you've got one more day to make up your mind," Gretchen said. "Then you are going to change back or eat. Your parents asked about you. We told them you were adjusting fine. I don't want to lie to them. You need to at least eat the food we provide for you." Max heard the clinking of the lid on the tray.

"I don't trust the food," she said. "I'll wait till I get out of here, if you don't mind."

"You aren't going to leave here, honey. You'll

either do what they want or you'll go into one of the rooms you saw in the treatment area."

"You mean the *morgue*?" Max said. She turned around to see Gretchen fixing her bed.

"They had to call it *something*, didn't they? We're dealing with a disease that keeps you alive when you should be dead. The morgue seems fitting."

Gretchen finished making the bed and laid the plastic out before her. Inside it was a beautiful, deep-red, strapless dress. The bodice was scalloped into a heart shape, and clear crystals accentuated the line. There were two layers of crinoline and chiffon at the hem. It looked tragic, deadly, and beautiful all at once. It reminded Max of herself.

"They wanted you to have something special for tonight. Corben Rothman sent this dress himself. It's going to be something you'll never forget."

Gretchen leaned in, tucked Max's hair behind her ear, then cupped her chin with her hand.

"Max, you don't remember the other world, but there were rituals and sweetness, even there. One of my earliest memories is of watching my youngest aunt get ready for a dance. She fixed her hair, put on perfume, makeup, and a gorgeous dress. I always dreamed I would have a night like that. It never happened. She died in the war. She went away to college and never came home. The world changed, and now we're here. Let me help you get ready."

Mesmerized by her beauty, her sadness, and her kindness, Max let Gretchen guide her to the bathroom, where she instructed her to shower. As the hot water cascaded onto Max's face and chest, she cranked the hot water knob, attempting to burn off all that held her in the facility.

Anxiety filled her as she guessed what Rothgen planned next. Were they going to put her in a pretty dress and then piss her off to the point where she would feed? Did they plan to strap her down and force flesh down her throat in high style?

As Max grabbed a towel from the rack, she shivered. Gretchen's eyes glistened with nostalgia as she stared through her. It occurred to her that this woman, who was only a couple of years older than her, had no clue what all of this meant.

MAXINE

Max knew what it meant.

It meant that regardless of what Max wanted, her childhood was over.

CHAPTER 14

Nancy Oregon felt a popping sensation first. Then a warmth filled her abdomen. Sweat beaded on her forehead, and she took long, deep breaths. Nancy's lungs burned, her stomach clenched. She rolled over to the side of the bed and vomited all over the floor.

She moaned. She looked for her call button. It was nowhere in sight. The clench in her stomach happened again, and she spewed blood all over herself and the bed. Bright red splats speckled her nightgown.

Nancy panicked. Her instinct was to get out of

the room. Her breathing increased. Blood dripped out of her mouth. She tried to sit up, but lost her balance. Her rigid body flopped out of the bed involuntarily. She landed on her stomach, and with all the effort remaining in her, dragged herself toward the exit.

Two feet from the door, her body stopped. Darkness set in, and Nancy felt nothing at all. Slowly, the sounds of the room shifted in the background, the light dimmed, and Nancy Oregon left her body.

"Ah, crap," Becca said. She picked up the phone next to the observation window and dialed Dr. Pennsylvania.

"What is it now?" Dr. Pennsylvania asked in his normal, annoyed-by-life voice.

"The Oregon girl. She turned total zombie. Big time," Becca panted.

"And you felt the need to call me about this right now?" he asked.

Becca could hear Dr. Pennsylvania fiddling with something on the other end of the phone.

"Well, well, what do you want *me* to do?" she stuttered.

"What do we do with zombies?" he asked, his voice more irritated.

"We eliminate them?" she asked, unsure of her answer.

"Exactly," Dr. Pennsylvania said. The scream of a young woman filled the phone for a second. Then Dr. Pennsylvania spoke again. "Follow the protocol, and don't call me with stupid questions again."

Becca grabbed the Zombie Protocol Manual and flipped to chapter sixteen, Zombie Activation. On the very first page, it instructed her to notify the reanimated's next of kin.

She dreaded calling Mr. Oregon. He was so dramatic about everything. She could probably eliminate the girl on her own with the captive bolt gun, but it would mean that she would have to get near her.

Dr. Pennsylvania would be pissed if she turned the incinerator on. It would leave the observation room unusable until the housekeeping team cleaned it.

A slam against the mirror interrupted Becca's train of thought. Nancy stood in front of her, covered in blood, eyes glazed over, and looking ready for her first meal. The protocol gave Becca one hour to eliminate the problem, or she could be eliminated with Nancy for breaking the rules.

Becca groaned in frustration as she slipped on the Kevlar-lined biohazard suit. She could call for backup, but everyone always complained about how she couldn't do anything by herself.

She would show them. The zombie would get a swift hit to the brain, and that would be the end of it. She'd call housekeeping for a cleanup, and everyone would praise her.

The weight of the captive bolt gun would require Becca to use both hands when aiming. She leaned into the door to Nancy's room, drew in one last breath, and opened it.

What was left of Nancy lunged toward her. Becca darted to the left, narrowly avoiding Nancy's grip. She thought the zombies were supposed to be slower than this. Before Becca

238

could collect her thoughts, Nancy slammed her against the wall. The room went black for a moment, but a sharp pinch to her arm startled Becca back to reality.

"Ow. You stupid jerk." Becca shoved Nancy across the room. She rubbed her arm. The Kevlar would protect her skin from breaking, but there'd be a nasty bruise, for sure. Nancy ran toward her again, unfazed by Becca's thwarts.

"Oh good grief," Becca said. She had been tired of Nancy since the minute she'd met the girl, and now, as a zombie, she was even less impressed.

She ran full force toward Nancy with the same enthusiasm. The two bodies collided over a pool of Nancy's blood.

There was a shuffling of feet that might have been comedic to Becca if it were happening to someone else, but at that exact moment, she regretted not putting on protective eyewear as the two fell to the floor.

They rolled in the blood, struggling to see who would land on top. Becca used the weight of the suit to roll on top of Nancy, grabbing the girl's head and bashing it in the floor.

Up and down it went until Becca heard the skull crack. She looked down at the muted maroon hair that had once been a golden blonde. She pushed herself up and walked to the door, but the knob wouldn't turn.

"What in the world," Becca mumbled.

All she wanted to do was get away from Nancy's body. She knew she hadn't caused the girl's first death, but she had the second one. She kicked the thick metal door in frustration. Now she'd have to call someone to open the door. Her plan was going all wrong.

Dr. Pennsylvania observed the med tech struggling with the reanimated corpse of the Oregon girl. He couldn't believe what he was seeing. The zombie was strong, fast, and more aggressive than any he'd ever seen.

The virus was mutating. If the zombies became more aggressive, it could lead to infiltration of the cities. A large red button on the wall near the mirror was within his hand's reach. It took him a fraction of a second to decide before he slammed it.

Flames flooded the room. The med tech thrashed back and forth. Dr. Pennsylvania felt a tinge of empathy as the Kevlar biohazard suit baked the med tech from the inside. But everyone was expendable, including a dim-witted med tech who couldn't wait for help in the cause of eliminating the infection.

CHARMING BOYS

"Wow. You look great," Gretchen said as she handed Max a hand mirror. Max inspected her freshly-cut bangs. She didn't see herself anymore. All she saw was a girl losing control of her life. Gretchen grabbed Maxine around the shoulders and looked in the mirror with her.

"Smile. You're beautiful, and you'll always be like this. The rest of us will get old and become useless. I wish I had your chance. I can't believe you've never tried bangs. They used to be a thing." She squeezed Maxine tighter. Blood raged through Maxine's body as she imagined stabbing Gretchen with the scissors the med tech had left on the counter. Her hand trembled as she picked up the small, sharp-tipped scissors. Gretchen touched the top of Maxine's hand.

"I know what you're thinking... they're short enough." Gretchen said, smiling with her mouth, but scolding with her eyes.

"You have no idea what I'm thinking right now," Max said. She slowed her breathing. There was no reason to let herself get upset and transition. Rothgen wouldn't care if she killed Gretchen. The ultimate goal would still be achieved. Max shook off Gretchen's hand and walked into the bedroom.

Gretchen scooted around Max and ran to the side of the bed to hold up two pairs of shoes. "So, do you want to wear heels or flats? They wanted heels, but since you've never worn them before, I thought you might want flats."

She smiled brightly at Max. Max didn't want to kill her, but her smile was enough to irritate anyone.

"Flats."

Max walked to the bed and sat down. Gretchen

244

put the flats down in front of her, and she gently slipped her feet inside. They were a perfect fit. They were black leather and felt soft on her feet. She wanted to take off the tight hosiery that bunched her toes together and feel the softness with her feet spread apart. She frowned. One more freedom taken away.

A light tap on the door interrupted her thoughts. Gretchen jumped with excitement. Max looked out the window. The sun was starting to set.

Gretchen was talking to one of the many handsome medical students that had come through to bring her meals. This one had beautiful, tan skin and dark eyebrows that put Max's old bushy brows to shame. This one had mentioned to Max that in his community they dressed differently, and some rules were different, while others were the same.

None of the other medical students had cared to share anything about themselves. The way he looked at Gretchen made Max believe that he might be the reason Gretchen was so eager to prove herself. If she could prove her value medically, could she show this one she was worth leaving this community and moving on to another as a doctor's wife?

Observing Gretchen's pretty smile and the flushing of her cheeks, Max couldn't blame her. She had felt that way about Nathan, even when the jerk treated her like crap.

The last time she had seen him, his eyes had held the same look of adoration, except he'd known that she was poisonous even before she did. He wouldn't come save her. She could kill him with the first rough kiss. Her life was at stake, and even her parents couldn't be bothered to help.

Max watched the two preoccupied outside the door. Rothgen had created a safe place for Max, or at the very least made it difficult for her to commit suicide. At least until Gretchen had screwed up and brought a pair of scissors into the room.

She had just finished stuffing the scissors between her breasts and down into her bodice when Gretchen walked back in the room. Her face was flushed, and she smiled wide, like a child who had been given a piece of candy.

"Arizona is amazing," Gretchen said, her voice

soft and dreamlike. "He's the only person in his family who lived through the war. He entered a community where he didn't know anyone. He didn't even speak English when he got there. Now he's going to be a doctor."

Gretchen stared at her own reflection in the mirror, and pushed a hair out of the way. She never noticed the scissors missing. Max smiled softly. She hoped that Gretchen achieved her goal of a happy marriage. Max didn't want to marry anyone or have children.

"Are you ready to go? I think after tonight you'll accept your new role," Gretchen said with glee.

"I'm as ready as I'm ever going to be," Max mumbled, taking shallow breaths so the scissors didn't stab her lung.

"Let's go." Gretchen held out her hand and led Max out of the bathroom, through her room, and out into the hallway. The two walked hand in hand. Max felt like a lamb being guided to her slaughter.

She had no idea where she was going or how to get out of the facility. There were no exit signs anywhere. The hallways all looked the same:

sterile white walls with white doors. There were signs on some of the doors, bearing names. She wasn't sure if they were names of patients who were actually ill, or kids like her.

Max didn't want to kill Gretchen, but she didn't want to be a slave to Rothgen any more than she already was. She focused on the closed doors and tried to orient herself as to which way she and Gretchen were going.

They headed toward double doors after what seemed to Max like they had been walking for half an hour. That's when she saw it: the sign above the door read, Morgue. Gretchen had taken the long way around to return Max back to an area she wanted nothing to do with.

The two entered the double doors. This time, curtains were drawn over all of the windows. This concerned Max. It must have shown on her face.

"Don't worry," Gretchen said reassuringly, "they didn't dispose of anyone. We try to get them to rest at night, just like everyone else. The rooms are darkened so they can relax."

Max nodded. She wondered if they were

heading back toward the exam room. The two walked past it and continued down the long, dim corridor. They moved toward a new set of doors and passed through.

Max felt the cool air as it hit her shoulders. The sky was a mixture of purple, red, and grey. She looked all around her. They were in a garden that was surrounded by three walls and the hospital. A soft, glowing light came from the right corner.

The girls walked down a path toward the twinkling light. Sitting on top of a picnic table was Ray, his elbows propped up on his thighs and his hands dangling at his calves. He looked relaxed and confident.

Max sensed the primal urge to be near him start to surge in her body. The feeling of acceptance and naturalness between them pressed her forward, urging her feet to move in his direction. She held her ground. He smiled at the sight of her. He'd known this would happen.

She looked away, focusing on the individual twinkling lights around the area. Ray stood up from the picnic table, produced four long-stemmed

249

roses, and held them out to her.

"It used to be customary to give a girl flowers on special occasions," Ray said. "These were specially delivered here, just for you. I picked them out. They're real. I didn't want you to have paper ones like the Moms like to make."

His smile contained a genuine sweetness. Max saw a dimple in his right cheek. It occurred to Max as she took the flowers from him and he accidentally touched her hand that Ray wasn't immune to her attraction, either.

"Thank you," she said, looking down at the ground.

Gretchen looked at both of them. "Okay, my job is done. Have a good night. I'll see you both later. I'm going to go find Dr. Arizona." She started to back away, smiled, and turned, walking quickly back into the facility.

Ray stepped closer. "You look beautiful. I wanted to say I'm sorry about what happened when you first got here." Max refused to look up. She saw Ray kicking the dirt with the tip of his shoe.

He continued. "I've been lonely for a long time,

Max. You have to understand: most of the girls I meet in here have already converted, and not everyone turns out to be pleasant once they change. There've been a few that went crazy. I know you think I'm horrible for starting to eat flesh before I had to, but given the option of going nuts and killing someone, I'm glad I made my choice. Yours isn't going to be easy."

Ray grabbed Max's hand and led her over to the picnic table. She wanted to keep looking at the ground, but Ray tipped up her chin. He looked in her eyes, and something happened between them. It was a synergistic effect that Max felt in her brain.

She didn't want to understand, empathize, or form any kind of alliance with this guy who had threatened her with torture over a week ago, but she felt the rush of chemicals moving her to be with him. He leaned in towards her. He put his lips on her cheek, and lightly brushed them slowly down to her mouth. She pulled back.

"Max, we can't help what comes natural between us. There's nothing wrong with it. If you don't feed tonight, you're going to turn back. At least enjoy tonight," Ray said.

Max jumped back from the table. Ray smiled softly, leaned back, and clicked a button. Music began to play softly. It was something Max had never heard before. The only music they were allowed to listen to was in school, and it didn't have words. This was a man's voice, and it sounded sultry, deep.

It reminded Max of the time her Mom had made a chocolate cake with three different types of chocolate and a pinch of coffee. The flavors had layered in her mouth, making her feel pleasure deep inside. The sound of the man's voice singing about the beautiful woman he loved evoked the feeling multiplied.

Ray walked over to her, grabbing her around the waist. He took her hand and held it up to his chest. He pulled her close, and her cheek touched his chin. He whispered in her ear, "Just go with it, Maxine. You won't regret this."

They danced under the twinkling lights until Max could see her breath. She was warm inside, even though her nose was cold. The two didn't speak for at least an hour. The viral attraction between the two was bliss when they were this close.

When the music stopped, Ray stepped away from her, removed his coat, and handed it to her. She put it on, even though her body was so hot that she hadn't complained of cold. Ray looked up at the dark sky, and Max looked up with him. The stars had never looked this bright. Ray grabbed her hand.

"I like to come out here and look at the sky. You know, it looked the same when the world was different. Every time the world has been different the stars stayed the same. I know you want to survive, Max. You're beautiful and strong now. It's not your fault you were born with the virus, but what you choose to do with it is up to you."

He kept focusing on the heavens. Max felt close to him, and sorry that he had never been allowed to be a child, like her. He'd always known the curse.

"I'm sorry about your sister," Max said quietly. "When we were elementary school she was one of the only kids that would play with me or invite me over to her house. She was a really nice person, and there was no way you could know what would happen to her."

Ray coughed. Max saw that his eyes were shining. She wondered if he wanted to cry.

"I wish with everything inside of me that Ellen wouldn't have died," he said, looking at her. "I was a little boy, and I didn't know what was wrong with me. She turned so unexpectedly. They don't turn like us. There's no switch for them. They're just like the zombies during the war. You're doing everyone a favor by separating yourself from them, even if you hate it."

Maybe he's right, Max thought. There was this magnanimous feeling between the two of them. She would never feel alone with Ray. The virus saw to it that they felt connected.

She put her hand in his and squeezed. Then she walked in front of him, stood on her tiptoes and kissed him. His lips were soft and gentle. He opened his mouth and let her lead. He put his hands on her waist and pulled her to him.

Max felt like she belonged, but she wasn't sure

254

how she was going to eat flesh. Maybe she could go back to being the plain little girl after one night of a fairytale? If Ray truly understood, he would let her go.

He pulled away and gently kissed her neck. She felt a shiver run down her spine. Her body naturally wanted to press itself closer to him. He squeezed one of her breasts. This pushed her over the edge, from feeling like she wanted to be with him toward a rush of fear that wasn't natural. She stepped back.

"I'm not ready for all of this," she said, breathing heavily. Ray nodded.

"I know it's a lot. I really think you're beautiful, and love the fact that you kissed me first this time, but the virus is really strong. It feels like it can take control of the situation." Ray stepped away. He scanned the area as though he were searching for a cue.

"Let's just go inside," he said. He held out his hand and led Max back into the facility, leaving the twinkling lights and the beautiful flowers on the table behind.

The two walked through the double doors, but

instead of going down the corridor to the lab rooms, Ray walked over to a set of elevators, pulled out a key, and placed it in a switch in the wall. The doors slid open and Ray walked in, pulling Max behind him.

"I have something for you upstairs in my living quarters." Ray pressed the button labeled two. Max felt a lurch in her stomach as the elevator went up. "I haven't lived at home with my Mom and Dad for several years. Ellen's Mom is scared of me. She has been for a long time, since even before Ellen turned."

The door slid open on the second floor. As soon as Max stepped off the elevator she could tell this area was different. There were black and white architectural photos of sky rise buildings from the past on the walls. The floors were hard wood. It almost looked like a home.

Each door was labeled with the name and title, and then underneath, which community the person was from. Max hadn't realized each community had a name.

The name on each door was distinctly male. It

shouldn't surprise her. Ray even admitted if she had been a boy she would have been pulled from school and trained early on for the medical program.

When they reached Ray's room, he opened the door, allowing Max to enter first.

Inside the room, Ray had light green walls, a tan comforter on his bed with light green fern print. When she turned around, she saw a wall full of books. Some of them were medical, but others were ones she had never seen before. She walked over to touch their spines. All of the books she had touched in her life were created by Rothgen. The leather bound spine on *Persuasion* by Jane Austen was especially worn.

"That book belonged to a lady who was having marriage troubles," Ray said. "She journaled in the margins. Having these books is one of the perks of being a doctor. You get things that the rest of the community doesn't have."

He sat down on his bed. Max pulled the book out and looked at the writing inside. She could see when the woman was upset versus when she was happy by the slant of her writing. The woman was discouraged because she couldn't be a good wife and mother.

"It seems like there were a lot of extremes in the old world," Ray pointed out. Then quietly asked, "Do you think you would have wanted to live in that place before the war?"

Max shrugged her shoulders, thumbing through the book. "I don't know." She had thought life before the war would have been amazing, being able to wear what you what want, do what you want, and be free to express yourself.

Ray touched her forehead softly and pushed back her hair. He kissed her below her ear. She felt a warm sensation crawl up her body. Her breathing quickened and her heart began to flutter.

She knew that if she became upset or excited, she would change. She had to stop this. Deep down she wanted to believe Ray was a nice guy and that he wouldn't push her, but he had acted like a crazed mad scientist in the lab. She pulled away. "Ray, what's so special about me? What's so important?"

Ray leaned in closer to her. "You're the first.

You didn't kill on your first conversion. You retaliated against someone who picked on you, but you never ate. Having that control makes you different from all of the rest of them. We both have developed in ways that Rothgen can work with to create better people with the virus."

"What do they plan to do with these people we create?" Max asked. "Are they going to make soldiers that scare people into submission just because they could bite them?"

Frustration was building inside of her. She wanted to kiss Ray again and forget all her troubles, but she felt like a lab rat. She had never been allowed to make any of her own decisions.

"It doesn't matter what they do with them," Ray said rubbing her back. "We get to stay safe if we do this."

"I don't feel safe here. Not at all," Max said. She rose from the bed and walked over to the window. "Two weeks ago, I thought I was just some weirdo. Now people are telling me that I need to start having babies? What kind of world is this?"

"You don't want to know the alternative. The

place outside of here is not safe for anyone. Not even us. You need to do this. I want you to do this. I'm tired of being alone. I'm eighteen, and all my life I've seen guys come through here and leave to become doctors in other communities. They have girlfriends now, and they'll get married someday. I don't want to live in this stupid hospital and be alone forever. My own Dad won't let me in his house."

Ray put his hands in his face and bent over. He took long, deep breaths. Max hoped he wouldn't turn on her. She assumed that the virus would keep him from tearing her apart, but she didn't want to find out.

Max walked over to Ray and rubbed his back gently. "I don't think they're going to let either of us leave this hospital. If we give them what they want, they'll start dissecting me or you or these beings they want us to create. Could you imagine having surgery all the time, being picked apart?" Max said, shuddering.

Ray unbuttoned his shirt. "I already know what that feels like." He exposed his chest to Max: a clean cut line that went from his mid-chest down to his belly button. The scars didn't stop there, he turned around so she could see the crisscrossed lines covering his back and spine.

She gulped. Ray had endured a lot. He didn't know he was a captive or a science experiment, because this was all he'd *ever* known.

"What's behind the border?" Max asked. "Is there a border around the community, or were you just telling me that to see if I was planning an escape?" She stared at Ray's chest. After closer examination, she saw he'd been cut open more than once.

"They call it Purgatory," Ray said. "Everything that lives there is neither living or dead. There's some biters still out there, and some of the communities threw their kids out instead of disposing of them like Rothgen instructed them to. These kids live without rules. There are many of them that are supposed to be more vicious than the mindless biters, because they can still think. They know what they are doing.

"There are rogue humans out there too—you

saw the videos in detention. They're worse than the biters. According to some of the med students, when you travel across Purgatory, you come in an armed car with guns. The students told me about the walls. I never went out there. I lied." Ray said. There was fear in his voice—Max heard it. He'd appeared cocky when she'd met him, but he was a scared child, and had chosen to live this way because of it.

Max could envision the world outside of the community. It did sound scary, but what were her options? Stay here and be the fearful, pregnant teen bride of Ray, or go out into Purgatory and try to survive? She wasn't going to die less painfully staying in the hospital, at the hands of Rothgen.

Wait—Nathan fit into all of this somewhere. How did he fit? Max felt she had nothing to lose. Nathan didn't look to be developing a rescue plan, so she needed to save herself.

"One day, I was at school and I saw you and Nathan talking in the chemistry lab. What was going on?" she asked. "Is he working with Rothgen?"

"His father is part of the underground to get people out of the community," Ray said. His face glowed with guilt. "I've known about the group for some time, because a kid was brought in here with a spinal injury. He ratted on them to me."

"What happened to the kid?" Max asked.

"After he told me what they were doing, I put him out of his misery. He'd never walk again. He asked for it. I figured having a piece of information no one else had would work to my advantage." Ray looked away from Max, toward the wall that held a map of the United States. "He told me Nathan was the person to talk to if you want to get out."

"So you wanted to get out?" Max asked.

"No. I wanted to know what Nathan knew about our kind," Ray said. "I wanted to kill him, but I held back. It was everything. He's been watching you for a long time. The day you saw us, we were fighting over your future. He wanted me to help get you out. I wanted him to let you go so that I wouldn't be alone. He called me selfish." Ray grabbed Max's hand and pulled her to his side. "I *am* selfish. I don't want to be alone."

MAXINE

"There are others like us, Ray. You could pick a girl closer to your age," Max said, brushing the side of his face. She tried to soothe him but nothing worked. He would either let her out of his own free will, or she would have to kill him.

CHAPTER 15

"Wuh-Ray, what're you doing?" Ellen Pennsylvania asked as she stood in her brother's doorway.

"Get out of here! I'm trying to play army men!" Ray yelled as he made two little green plastic figurines battle one another.

Ellen toddled across the bedroom and pulled herself onto the twin-sized bed. She stared, fascinated at her big brother and his toys. After much deliberation, she snatched an army tank from its platoon. It was twice the size of her hand, but she squealed with glee at having obtained it.

265

She pointed the tank's gun at a platoon of men. "Pow, pow, pow, pow!"

"Stop! You can't kill the army men." Ray protested.

"Why, Bubba?" Ellen asked.

"Because, the army men saved us," he explained. "They killed all the zombies. They don't kill each other no more. We never say bad things about them or the Rothman family. They fixed everything. Okay?"

Ellen stuck out her bottom lip. "I don't like zombies. They're scary. They eat people."

"I know. But they're all gone," Ray reassured her. "Nothing will ever hurt us now."

"Can we play Kill the Zombies instead?" She bounced up and down enthusiastically.

"Ellen, I have a serious battle going on here. I don't want to play with you right now." Ray scooped up his men and turned away from her.

Tears welled in her eyes. She hurled the army tank at Ray's head. "You're mean!"

Ray turned to his little sister and smacked her leg. Ellen lunged at him and smacked his face.

Instinctually, Ray grabbed her arm and bit so hard he drew blood.

Ellen wailed with such force she rolled off the bed then landed with a thud on the carpeted floor. She shook herself off and went in search of their parents, baying all the way.

Ray crawled under his bed. His father would come for him. All of the toys would be gone, and he wasn't sure if his Dad would spank him. The last time he'd been swatted was over spitting on his stepmother. He laid in wait, listening to Ellen scream. Tears rolled down Ray's face as he waited for the inevitable.

It was dawn when Dr. Pennsylvania pulled his son out from under his bed. He examined the boy's translucent skin and the blue squiggly lines that ran up and down his temples. As he was prone to do, he checked for a pulse.

Ray's eyes fluttered open. "Daddy?"

"Good morning," Dr. Pennsylvania said. He swallowed hard and tried to control his breathing. He leaned over and kissed Ray on the forehead.

MAXINE

Ray looked up at his father with red-rimmed eyes. "Am I in trouble?"

"No, son. But you're going to go live at the hospital." Dr. Pennsylvania stroked his son's hair. "The folks I work for from the City Upon the Hill think it might be better for you there."

"I'm not sick, Daddy! Don't make me go there. I will miss you and Ellen too much." Ray shook his head until he became dizzy. He leaned on his father for balance.

"We do what they tell us. Remember?"

"Uh huh," Ray replied.

"Pick out your favorite toys, and then we'll go." Dr. Pennsylvania got up and left the room.

Ellen peeked her head in, "Wuh-Ray, Daddy said you are leaving."

"Yeah. I'm going to go live at the hospital." Ray shoved his favorite teddy bear in his knapsack.

"Why?" Ellen said. She waddled over to her brother and hugged him around the waist.

Ray squeezed his little sister. "Because we do what the army men and Rothgen tell us to do, always."

"That is dumb. You should be with people who love you. *I* love you, Wuh-Ray."

SPECIAL AND SHINY

"You don't understand yet. You're special, and unless you allow them to replicate you, there probably won't be a chance to fix what has happened," Ray said. He let go of her hands, stood up, and walked over to the windows.

"You won't do this without a fight will you?" he asked.

"No, I don't *want* to do this. My body and mind have not adjusted to the rapid changes." She sat on the bed, her arms crossed with determination.

"You really don't care if you turn back into a little creepy blob of nothing?" Ray turned away from the mirror and looked at her again.

"I want to be free to be myself," Max said. "This is what the virus is doing to me." She looked in the mirror on the back of Ray's bedroom door. Her bosom overflowed from the top of the dress. Her hair was so healthy and beautiful. *She* was beautiful, and she would miss it.

"No, this is who you *would have* been if the virus wasn't depleting your body," Ray said, moving toward her. "The person you are without the flesh is because of the virus. Not this. If you were a normal girl, this is what you would have grown up to look like." He pulled Max up. "You are supposed to look like this: vibrant, healthy, gorgeous."

Max looked at herself again. Her legs looked long in the short dress. Her waist was small. She was a glowing girl—or she *would have been* a glowing girl, if life had not dealt her the virus. Of course, if there were no virus, the world she lived in wouldn't even exist. Ray bent his head and kissed her shoulder.

"Being overweight didn't make me nothing,"

Max told him. "I was always someone. I don't want to be beautiful. I don't care if I'm healthy. I don't want to be a slave to Rothgen. Let me go, Ray. If you want to come with me—we're two smart people, we could get along in Purgatory. I know it." Max didn't plead, but the tone of her voice begged for Ray to consider all the options.

"I can't leave here," Ray said. "There are more reasons than you know, but if you really won't stay, if you absolutely can't bear the thought of having my children and living here… I'll do for you what I did for that kid who lay dying on the table."

His voice was calm, but not cold. It reminded Max of when she'd been a child and the doctor had told her he was giving her a shot, and it would only hurt a little. She wasn't sure what Ray meant.

She turned to him and asked, "What're you going to do? Kill me?" She looked up into his eyes. They were filled with more emotion than his voice had been.

Ray's tried to speak, but it came out in a whisper. "No, I'm going to let you go."

Max was shocked at his words. Would he really

let her go?

"Nathan and I had an agreement. He would give me until the last day before you are to turn back to convince you to stay here with me. If you agreed, he would let it alone. If you didn't want to stay under any circumstances, then I would help you leave. You are really beautiful. In more ways than you know."

Ray leaned down and kissed her. His hopes and dreams of some kind of normal life were going to disappear. He deserved that last moment before it was all gone.

Max gently pushed him away. "I'm ready to go, and the longer we prolong it, the more it will hurt you. I know there is a connection between us, but I don't know how much of it is the virus or real feelings. It has to hurt like hell for me to choose a life out in Purgatory over living in comfort with you. It's just something I have to do."

Ray nodded.

"I know," he said, "but I wasn't kidding. Any feelings you have for Nathan have to be left behind. I'm not saying that out of jealousy. I'm saying it to save his life. He knows he can't kiss you or give you what I can. It will kill him."

Ray squeezed her to the point her lungs felt like they would burst. He buried his face in her hair. She felt his breath. Ray would probably never have an opportunity to be close to a female again. If she couldn't have Nathan, Ray would never have a normal girl, either. She squeezed back, giving him the warmth and affection that he desired.

Max pulled back and looked up at him. "So how are we going to get me out of here?"

Ray smiled mischievously, though his eyes held sadness. "Well, it involves you stabbing me with those scissors you've had stuck between your boobs all night. Do you think you'll have a problem stabbing a guy who threatened to cut you up a week ago if you didn't have his kids?"

Max swallowed hard. She knew Ray wasn't all bad. He was one messed-up guy from all the crazy things that had happened to him over his short life, but he wasn't evil.

"I definitely wouldn't have a problem stabbing that guy. It's *you* I'll have a problem doing it to."

She hugged him one last time.

Ray gently pulled away. "Let's bust you out of this place."

CHAPTER 16

"Are we alone?" Esther Hampshire said as she walked through the rows of vacant lockers, searching for eavesdroppers.

"Yeah, we're fine. Are you going to tell me what is going on?" Marie Washington said, unimpressed with Esther's paranoia. She sat on the bench and filed her fingernails.

Esther laid down on the bench in front of Marie and covered her eyes with her arm. "What's *wrong*? Two of our friends are gone, and we have no clue where they are. And that creepy Maxine morphed into one of the most gorgeous girls we've ever seen. She's gone, too!" She rolled over on her side and stared at Marie. "You don't think that is a problem?"

"Don't you remember what your dad told you?" Marie sat her nail file down on the bench, crossed her legs, and placed her hands in her lap. "Well, *do* you?"

"Ugh." Esther jumped up from the bench and paced in front of Marie. Her pleated plaid skirt flapped back and forth in time to her steps. "I don't think he's right. You can't just pretend like people never existed. Like everything is okay when it isn't! Look at Mr. Oregon. He comes in here every day and doesn't talk about Nancy. She's completely erased. Ellen? I tried to ask Dr. Pennsylvania about her at last inspection. Nothing. What if we are next?"

"Honestly, we are nothing like Ellen, Nancy, or that Mess-a-shit-etts girl. All of them had their issues. Ellen was a loudmouth, Nancy a weakling, and that Mess-a-shit-etts? What *wasn't* wrong with her? Did you ever think Rothgen had a reason to get rid of them?"

Marie stood up and looked around the dirty locker room. "This place smells. I need to get out of here. I think we need to continue to be outstanding, beautiful McCarthy citizens. Nothing will happen to us, then."

"Something is going on. I can feel it. I don't think Rothgen has our best interests at heart." Marie's eyes welled with tears. "What happens if they take us all?"

Marie walked toward the locker room exit, stopped, and turned around. "If Rothgen wants us dead, we'll be dead. We'll be whatever they want us to be. Don't you get that?"

Esther pulled the bottom of her sweater up and wiped off her face. "Don't we get any choices?"

Marie laughed. "You *do* get a choice. Do you want to be a secretary, a med tech, or a bride, after high school?"

Esther pulled her sweater down and mumbled, "I just don't want to be dead."

ESCAPE PLAN

Ray pointed below his left collarbone. He had informed Max it would be the perfect place to stab without damaging any of the major blood vessels or nerves to his arms, but it would hurt like hell, making it plausible that she could escape.

It was quick, and Ray actually did pass out from the pain. Max watched as the blood pooled around his body, then walked out the door.

Ray had assured Max that he would be okay. He was supposed to have her returned to her room by the morning, converted and on their way to creating the legion of Rothgen's newest soldiers.

Someone would check on him, and he calculated that he could afford to lose some blood, since he had just fed earlier in the day. But what if they didn't believe his story? After he had been so compliant, she couldn't imagine them torturing him.

She followed his directions to the letter. Now that he'd explained the system of the building, she was able to navigate her way to the rendezvous point.

Max stood out in the cold, wearing a pair of Ray's medical scrub pants, a t-shirt, and his suit jacket. Compared to most guys Ray had a small frame, but even in his clothes, Max felt like a child playing dress-up.

The crisp fall morning air was evidenced by the mist from her breath. She found herself trembling as she waited for the semi-truck that would take her away from the facility.

Nathan's father delivered goods to this loading dock every morning. Max was supposed to hide behind the garbage cans until the last dock worker went inside, and then jump into the trailer. Ray had told her that Nathan would be waiting at the very back of the truck, and she would hide in a compartment until they were out of the community.

She felt guilty at the excitement of seeing Nathan again.

The metal from the dumpster was moist and cold against her skin. After twenty-four hours without sleep, her body hurt, black spots clouded her vision, and chills ran down her spine.

She watched quietly as each box was removed from the back of the trailer and carried into the hospital's loading dock. Max had never met Nathan's father. She expected him to be a big, burly man who looked gruff, but when he jumped from the truck, his small, thin frame, balding head, and the bags under his eyes made him look defeated.

He looked like some of the other adults did when they thought no one was watching: as if the life had been sucked out of them. Nothing left to look for, or believe in. Of course, she also knew from talking to Nathan that his only daughter had been shot dead when she wasn't in her zombie form.

A broad-shouldered man who looked about twenty stepped out of the back and yelled out, "Last one! Let's get this done so we can get some coffee."

Two other men walked over, and assisted him with pushing the last box off the trailer. Max waited patiently as Nathan's father and the three men walked inside the building.

Nathan's father intentionally left the gate open wide enough for her to crawl in. Now, she just needed the courage to run across the dock, slide under, and run to the back of the trailer without being seen. She wasn't sure how the dock worker hadn't seen Nathan or the compartment. She really hated the idea of being in the back of the trailer in the dark. What if they caught her? Her self-doubt was given little time to spare.

Max scanned the area, looking for any guards or stragglers, but the cold air of the morning kept them inside. As she ran, she remained conscious of where Ray had told her the camera was, and darted toward the back of the truck. The flats from the night before made small patting sounds as she ran across the dock.

When she scooted herself under the sliding door, she felt a hot, searing pain in her left leg. She rolled into the bed of the truck and looked down to see that her scrub pants had ripped open, exposing a small, bleeding wound. She wasn't hemorrhaging, but it was the type of scrape that burned to the core of her belly.

She gritted her teeth and took a deep breath. All she needed was to turn in the dark, where Nathan was somewhere waiting for her.

She rolled over on her belly and pushed herself up. The light stopped about two feet into the bed of the truck. Beyond that was total darkness. She took a couple of slow, deep breaths and started walking toward the back end.

She'd been instructed to tap three times on the back of the trailer to notify Nathan that she was there. The walk seemed to go on forever. Even though she knew there probably wasn't anything scarier than her in the back of the truck, it felt like, at any moment, something would reach out and grab her.

The beating of her heart made her deaf to anything around her. The virus began to pulse through her veins. The dull, aching pain of her fingernails feeling as though they were about to pop off seemed to be an ordinary symptom that she would transition.

Part of her thought the virus was trying to fight for survival now that her final day in her new body was beginning. She felt weak and began to move faster. Before she could anticipate the end of the trailer, her head collided with something hard.

CHAPTER 17

"Ladies first," medical student Arizona said as he opened the door to the morgue with a grand, sweeping motion.

"Thank you, doctor," Gretchen said. Her cheeks turned pink. She knew it was a matter of time before he was an official doctor, but it didn't hurt to practice.

"You're welcome." He gave her a large, wide smile, showing his perfect white teeth.

The two walked down the stark hallway, each aware of the magnetic attraction between them. Gretchen kept quiet. She'd been trained from a young age to keep her mouth shut when it was important.

"Do you want to go check on her?" Dr. Arizona asked.

Gretchen let out a sigh of relief. "Is it obvious that it is the only thing on my mind?"

"Yeah."

They laughed and turned down the hall to Maxine's room.

As they reached it, Gretchen placed her hand on Dr. Arizona's arm and squeezed slightly. "Let me go in first. She might be really embarrassed after her first time." She winked at him, then opened the door.

"How do *you* know what it would feel like? You're not supposed to *even* kiss in McCarthy unless it is with your betrothed, right?"

Gretchen giggled. "Well, some rules are meant to be bro—" She stopped giggling and looked around the room. Nothing was out of place, and that was a problem.

"Does it look like she slept in here last night?" she demanded.

He stood silent, as if unsure what to say.

Gretchen instructed him, instead: "Move. We gotta get to Ray's room. Maybe they got along a little better than we hoped."

Dr. Arizona followed Gretchen as she charged out of the room.

"Do you want me to close the door?" he asked.

"Sure, whatever. Move your ass!" she yelled behind her.

Gretchen knew one thing for sure: Ray and Maxine were not going to ruin her chance of getting married and having the life she wanted. As she ran down the hallway, Gretchen struggled with worst case scenarios she'd have to explain to Dr. Pennsylvania. What if Ray had dissected his date? Maxine had accidentally ripped his throat out? Or the worst scenario of all: they'd both decided to abandon the project altogether.

Best case ideal scenario: they'd decided to have sex before they needed to and triggered some other weird reaction in Maxine that would work to Rothgen's benefit.

As she neared Ray's door, she slowed to a walk.

She didn't want to scare the kids if they'd fallen asleep. The door was cracked open, and Gretchen carefully pushed it wider.

"Ah hell. Arizona!" Gretchen yelled.

She examined Ray's shoulder. Her first instinct was to pull the pointed scissors from his clavicle, but she thought better of it.

She grabbed a washcloth from his bathroom, ran cold water over it, and placed it on his forehead. She assessed the room, looking for a sign of Maxine. The girl was gone.

Then she saw it: her dress was crumpled in the corner.

She couldn't contain herself; without thinking, she smacked Ray across his face.

Ray's eyes fluttered. "Whaa?"

Gretchen pushed the scissors further in his flesh.

"Ow!" Ray opened his eyes wide and looked up at Gretchen. "What're you doing?"

"You little incompetent prick! Where the hell is she?" Gretchen hissed.

She twisted the scissors in further.

Ray laughed. "You think I'd tell that easy?"

Gretchen jumped on top of Ray, yanked the scissors out of his chest, then stabbed him with them.

The boy screamed with terror and pain.

"Get this crazy witch off of me!" Ray screamed.

Arizona leaned in the doorway, "Kid, you aren't the only one who gets lonely. Give her what she wants, or I'll finish what she started."

Gretchen stopped and turned to Arizona. "Are you saying what I think you're saying?"

"Yeah, I need a wife who won't let anything get between her and what she wants."

Gretchen cried tears of joy. Ray cried tears of shame. Arizona walked over and stood over them both.

"If we don't know where the girl went in sixty seconds, I'm going to kill you."

"I'll tell you where they went, just get off me." Ray said in defeat.

GOODBYE, BOY FRIEND

Max heard the vibration before she felt it: a hum rang through her brain. Gradually it began to shake her body, and then she was awake. She felt the sharp pain at the front of her head and touched it. She pulled back from the round mound.

I must have hit my head when I passed out, she thought. She looked up. All around her were latches, and each latch held clothes, backpacks, shoes, and weapons. She looked across from her and saw Nathan sitting on a small crate like the one she was on, his face relaxed and his eyes closed. She leaned slightly forward and nudged his knee with her shoe.

"Hey, wake up," she said gently, trying not to scare him.

"Hmmm?" he replied in a drowsy stupor.

It took Nathan a moment to awaken. Once he did, the look on his face made Max feel relieved. He was happy to see her. She could see it in the way his eyes glistened and he smiled at her.

He leaned over and hugged her, and she felt the warmth of his body. The feeling she had for him was so different from the way she felt with Ray. The feeling with Ray was beyond her control, but with Nathan, it was her choice.

Her heart ached as she thought about her ability to choose; she would also have to choose to stay away from him, so that she didn't infect him. Max pushed him back and smiled.

"Thanks for believing in me," she said.

"I wanted to give you the option to leave if you wanted," Nathan said. "It would be hard for *anyone* to leave the power, security, and vanity of what Rothgen could give. I wasn't sure you would make it." He looked away from her, as if ashamed of his doubt in her character.

"There's no power in being the creator of a new race of humans. And for what? So I can look like Esther and the rest of the girls in high school forever?" Max said.

No one at Rothgen had been exceptionally cruel to her, but she remembered the man on the video running away from the soldiers even as they shot him down. Rothgen wanted to finalize their total control over humanity. She couldn't be part of that no matter how uncomfortable her life became.

"Besides, Ray showed me what Rothgen can do to you even when you *do* cooperate." Max shuddered, remembering Ray's chest. Rothgen must have operated on him dozens of times.

"I don't feel too sorry for him," Nathan said, crossing him arms defensively. His face curled up like he had eaten something sour. "That guy is only looking out for himself."

"He let me go," Max said. "He even let me stab him so that it looked like I'd attacked him."

It was hard to defend Ray to Nathan. One had wanted to keep her captive, while the other wanted to set her free. Ray had his problems, but he'd had the foresight to accept who he was even as a boy, and try to control the virus. He'd let her make her choice even though it meant he would be alone.

Nathan eyed Max's scraped knee. He reached behind his back and pulled a first aid kit from a compartment, then threw it at Max. She opened the box, grabbed an antiseptic wipe, and wiped off her scrape. She examined it; it was superficial, which was probably what made it sting so much. She placed a large adhesive bandage over the wound. It would be better soon enough.

"I'm sorry," Nathan said. "Ray just bothers me. He wanted to keep you there to be his teen bride or some crap. I was worried he would hurt you, but instead you're here and you have some kind of loyalty to him. I wanted to save you and I failed."

"It was no one's job to save me but myself," Max said. "I'm so thankful Ray changed his mind, but I was leaving that facility whether either of you had a plan or not." Both Ray and Nathan had wanted to be heroes, but in the end, Max knew she had to be her own heroine.

Nathan nodded and cleared his throat. "Okay, let's get you started on everything you're going to need to know about Purgatory." He looked down at his watch. "We've got about three hours."

A large black and green backpack was placed between them. Nathan pulled its contents out of the bag piece by piece, meticulously inspecting them for defects. At the bottom of the bag, Nathan pulled out a pair of camouflaged green pants with multiple pockets, an olive colored shirt with waffle-shaped indentions, and a T-shirt in a lighter shade of green. He tossed the items to Max.

"Change. You're going to need these out there. It's old military stuff from before the war," Nathan said as he inspected a long blade with his thumb.

Max stared at him. "Are you going to turn around or what?"

Nathan chuckled and turned around. Max pulled off the thin scrub pants and slipped on the heavy military pants. They sagged on her.

Max pulled off the white T-shirt that Ray had given her. Part of her wanted to keep it, but she knew it wasn't practical. She slipped the waffle-textured shirt on.

It felt scratchy against her skin, but he guaranteed it would help keep her warm. The green T-shirt was tight across her chest, but she knew why, now. She threw the torn scrub pants at Nathan, and he turned around, nodding his head in approval.

"Okay, so let's go through this stuff. All of this can be replaced if you scavenge, but it won't be easy. Different groups control the area. You're going to be dealing with kids like you who have never eaten flesh, flesh-eaters, zombies, and rogue humans.

"We try to work with those who've never eaten flesh the most. They are the most calm and predictable. Flesh-eaters are beautiful, but cold and prone to rages. They don't see themselves as human at all. Humans hate them and they think of all of you the same as zombies. Then there are still zombies out there. They kind of roam the areas searching for anything they can devour, but they are not attracted to your kind. The virus senses its own and won't allow them to attack you."

Nathan sat with a dagger in his hand, rolling it back and forth.

"What?" Max asked.

"I wish I could go with you. Protect you from all the horrible things you're about to see and be part of."

Max bit her lip and nodded slightly. She agreed. She wished he could come with her as well. She could only imagine the people she was about to meet.

"Another thing: the kids you're gonna meet didn't grow up the same way we have. There's going to be kids who talk totally different, have a different understanding of how Rothgen communities work, and different ideas on how people should behave."

He pulled out a can opener and tested it by opening a can of beans. He flipped the end of the can opener to a spoon and dug into the pinkish-red syrup. Max winced. It looked as bad as the girl eating flesh in the laboratory. Nathan pushed the can towards Max, and she reluctantly accepted it.

"Get used to it," he advised her. "The only fresh

things you will be eating shortly will be rabbits and squirrels." He smiled a little, trying to make light of the fact that after tomorrow, Max would have to eat raw wild animal flesh just to keep her body alive.

The two continued to dig through the pack. Max wasn't sure she could carry it for long, but Nathan assured her his father knew what he was talking about. He'd even hiked out the trails himself, to connect with kids who could help create an escape route.

The last thing placed back in the bag was what seemed to be half a commissary's worth of candy. Nathan explained that candy of any kind was invaluable. Hopefully, it would help her trade until she learned to navigate her new world.

Nathan opened a candy bar and handed half to Max. She devoured the chocolate quickly, hoping Nathan hadn't noticed she'd set the beans aside. His wavy blonde hair fell messily over his forehead. He leaned back with a content smile on his face as he nibbled at the chocolate.

She leaned her head against the rough wooden

wall and stared at him. She had so many questions to ask him, about his feelings for her and why he'd chosen to help her. He could have let Rothgen keep her, or worse, let her turn.

Was it all just about his sister, or did he really care for her? There had been times in school when he'd been so cruel that she'd wanted to beat him, but now he was kind and caring. She had to say what was on her mind.

"Before, I turned, why did you treat me like crap?" Max asked.

Nathan lay back further against the wall and closed his eyes. Max saw he was trying to distance himself from her. He took slow, deep breaths.

Max waited until her patience was exhausted. Then she picked up Ray's old shirt and threw it at Nathan's face.

"Answer my question. Seriously, why did you treat me like crap for so long?" Max asked. There was an edge to her voice. She wasn't going to turn, but she was irritated enough by his silence that she might just hit him while she was in her normal form.

Nathan stayed quiet.

"What made you treat me like dirt? Huh? Can't tell me now? Are you ashamed?" Max felt her face getting hot, and her heartbeat filled her ears.

Finally, Nathan sat up and looked her in the eyes.

"I liked you before, and it freaked me out," he said, fixing her with a serious stare. "I thought you were beautiful even when you were bigger and when everyone else thought you were plain. I thought there was something wrong with me for wanting you over all of the other girls. The way you looked isn't what I'm supposed to want."

Max wasn't sure if it was the sweetest or most horrible thing anyone had ever said to her. She hoped he would stop there, but he continued.

"I thought to myself: *why do you want the one girl who's incredibly self-conscious and extremely intelligent? Could you even kiss her?* Then I thought about what I would do if we could go out on a date. Do all the things my Dad said kids used to do. I had dreams about you, and it made me feel so weird that I wanted to make you feel bad. I don't know that girls get the same kind of dreams that guys do…"

"I don't think we have them while we're sleeping," Max mumbled as the redness came back to her cheeks. "I think we daydream about the guys we want all day long."

"Then the next thing I know, you're at school and you've changed to the kind of girl I always thought you looked like anyway. It messed me up. I knew we were never going to be together. I'd seen the traits my sister had for a long time." Hopelessness crossed his face.

Max had to laugh a little. He'd been carrying more torment than she'd known. He was correct: they'd never be together. All the times she'd stared into space and dreamed about him kissing her lips would never happen in reality.

In the end, he was a little immature, but the good guy she'd hoped he was. Before she could stop herself, she leaned forward and crawled into his lap. She hugged him, and whispered into his ear.

"I want you to remember two things: me just like this, and it isn't okay to take your problems out on girls. So, the next time you find a girl you like, be the good guy."

She slapped him lightly on his chest then squeezed him tightly. She heard him sigh. He squeezed back and kissed her cheek. She knew that though her mouth ached for him to kiss her on the lips, she would never want to chance him becoming infected.

She curled her legs up close to her chest, and Nathan wrapped his arms all the way around her protectively, and leaned back. The hum of the tires on the road and gentle swaying of the trailer lulled them both back to sleep.

CHAPTER 18

Justin Texas drove south on the long stretch of highway from what had once been called Flagstaff, Arizona towards the remains of Phoenix. Mile after mile, all his eyes could see were thin layers of red clay dirt.

Occasionally the wind blew and evidence of civilization appeared; a glint of metal from a gas station sign glared like a beacon until he passed it, and just like hope that a decent life was still out there, it was gone.

He estimated that the Nevadas and the Massachusetts girl had a six-hour head start on him. It should only take two hours to get to Phoenix from Flagstaff, but the truck driver would've had to pull over and manipulate the truck's tracking device, and the road wasn't ideal anymore.

Rothgen didn't have motivation to keep the roads drivable for the average Joe in a sedan. He grumbled, *They could have least given me one of the military jeeps.*

He had a simple goal: retrieve the Massachusetts girl and get rid of the Nevadas, making it look like a hijack of the truck. It would tidy up things nicely.

It would also double as a cautionary tale: Without Rothgen's protection you would die. Sure, they could have sent a team out, but what he was about to do wasn't going to look pretty, and the fewer witnesses, the better.

He was far enough out of the mountains. They could have turned west and headed north toward Cottonwood or southeast toward Pine; he wasn't going to know for sure unless the tracking beacon still worked.

He pulled up his GPS and studied the screen. It

definitely had to be in this area, because the last known active spot was on the exit to Camp Verde. Nevada wouldn't have taken her down to Phoenix; she'd be dead before sunrise—like *real* dead. No half-zombie bullshit.

He pulled over to the side of the road. Driving eighty miles an hour down the highway wasn't helping him figure out where to go, and he needed to get out and stretch his legs anyway.

He pulled over at the rest area, facing out over the valley. He looked northwest and then to the southeast.

Which way would *he* have taken a kid who was as about as capable as a caged bird with clipped wings? He closed his eyes and took a couple of deep breaths. *Use your gut*, he told himself.

They'd gone toward Pine.

The Nevadas had moved her down away from the forest, and there were probably more kids like her closer to New Mexico, since the community of Grant was located at the north end of what had once been Albuquerque.

It was a community full of what once were

called Native Americans that Rothgen had designated to be ruled by non-native overlords. He found it repulsive, living in a community structured after a paranoid time in U.S. history with the platitudes of commercialism and perfections, but it wasn't the same as being forced back into world worse than the reservations prior to the end of the world.

There would be people from Purgatory in that area who'd escaped from Grant. People who'd be okay with helping a half-zombie rather than bow to a new government that had crapped on them worse than the one before.

Of course, if she traveled too far, she'd be up near where what was once Santa Fe, which was a fantasy land of saloons and cowboys of the Wild West who used to be Wall Street Tycoons. What a mess.

If he was wrong? No loss. He'd turn around and hunt them down the other way. That girl would be dead no matter what.

THE ROAD STOPS HERE

Three rough raps to the back of the hidden space echoed in the container. During their nap, Max's legs had drifted to the floor from exhaustion, but she lay with her head on Nathan's chest. Both awoke with a start.

Nathan looked into her eyes mournfully. They both knew there were only moments left to spare. He hugged her one more time, and she squeezed back. Tears threatened to fall from her eyes, and she blinked rapidly.

Nathan pushed her up, and she stood off to the side while he opened the door. His father smiled at both of them as he shined a bright light into the small area.

"Maxine, are you ready?" Mr. Nevada asked.

"Does it matter if I say no?" she asked.

Mr. Nevada laughed softly and shook his head. "No, it doesn't. You're Rothgen's most wanted. Even if you turn back tonight, they won't forget you escaped."

His face became solemn as he looked from Nathan to Max. "After today, you can never go back to McCarthy. Do you understand? You can't go to any of the other communities, either, no matter what the other kids tell you. They'll shoot you on sight at the walls."

Nathan touched her arm. "Yeah, all of the communities are named for people from the past, in my opinion some of them not very nice. The next community over from us is Kennedy. Then there's Roosevelt, Grant, and Fillmore, that I'm sure of. Dad knows the names of the rest."

"The important thing is, no matter where the kids are from, figure out their motives. Do they want to go back? Are they flesh-eaters? Are they

KATIE CORD

outcasts who are going to turn into full-blown zombies? There are very few humans you can really trust out here, so don't get too close to them. You understand?" Mr. Nevada asked.

Max nodded her head. "Yes sir, Nathan told me."

"Good. Nate, grab her backpack and let's go."

Nathan pulled out a large round leather loop that held small silver pieces. It took her a moment to realize they were bullets. He situated himself, then grabbed her pack. When Nathan stepped out, Mr. Nevada came in and pulled a machete and small gun off the wall. He pointed for Max to go out before him.

"We're going to hike you out to a meeting point, and from there, you'll travel with some of the other kids who're working with us. Ordinarily, I would encourage you to stick with them, but you're going to be a target, so listen to them and let them help you get into Purgatory as far as you can go. The kids don't tell me everything that goes on out there. I guess it's their way of protecting me."

Mr. Nevada stepped out of the hidden

compartment, then placed a large piece of plywood over the door. The three walked toward the light at the end of the truck. Nathan threw his gun and Max's pack down, then helped her out. Mr. Nevada slowly climbed down.

Max looked around, expecting to see greenery like that inside of the community, but instead it was desolate. The ground was red, brown, and yellow. There was no life that she could see. On the horizon, the skyline resembled that of one of the old cities.

"You're not going there," Nathan said as he handed Max the pack. "At least not yet."

She swung the large green bag onto her back. She adjusted the weight and fell in line behind Mr. Nevada. The new found strength was one thing she would miss more than anything. Lifting heavy objects and walking without being breathless were things she never thought she would be able to do.

"Before the war, there were many beautiful cities, women, and ways of living," Mr. Nevada said over his shoulder. "I lived in a place called Las Vegas. I programmed all the machines for people to play games on for money. My first wife was a photographer. She photographed some of the most beautiful things you could think of. It's what got her infected. She had to take pictures of the damn zombies. We didn't know what to do, with her being pregnant and the world coming to the end." Mr. Nevada became silent.

Max had not dealt with the fact she didn't know who her real parents were. She was thankful that the two she'd lived with for so long had protected her for as long as they had. She wondered if her mother missed her. Was she okay with her father helping Rothgen to subdue her daughter?

"Do you know why my dad helped Rothgen?" she asked.

"Pretty much the reason we all help Rothgen. You either do it or get fed to the zombies," Mr. Nevada said.

"But *you're* helping me. Why couldn't he do what you're doing?" She wished her dad was like Nathan's.

"Every man has a role to play in this new world. Your dad knew you were intelligent and you'd either play Rothgen's game or you'd figure out a way to escape. Either way, your father has a much more important job than I do: trying to regulate those Suits and keep the folks in the City Upon the Hill from experimenting on us any more than they already have."

Mr. Nevada never stopped walking. He looked around the area and followed an invisible line up into the reddish-brown rocks. As the three walked closer, Max saw small shrub brushes. A rabbit jumped out from one and hopped in between the large formations.

"What's the name of the main community?" Max asked.

"The City Upon the Hill. Don't get me started. I assume it's because the Rothmans believe in old-fashioned values," Mr. Nevada said.

Max became quiet as she pushed herself up on the rocks. They were warm from the sun. As the elevation increased, the horizon broadened. There was nothing as far as the eye could see except the sandy ground, rock formations, the semi-truck a little off in the distance, and the outline of the broken city.

She pushed herself to keep walking. Her body was tired. The time was nearing for her body to return to the state she'd always known. It would be a sad goodbye, but that was the price she was willing to pay to not lose her humanity. Nathan came up behind her and hugged her again.

"You're going to be okay," he said. "The team we are setting you up with will help you as much as they can without compromising our mission."

"What *is* your mission?" Max asked. "Do you plan to save every one of us little infected beings?" She knew there had to be more to all of this than just saving kids. There had to be a bigger plan in place.

Mr. Nevada turned around and looked at Max, his face hard and intense. "Max, we want to save everyone and take back our world. The more kids we find like you, the better. You can kill the zombies without fear of being bitten. You can choose not to feed, and eventually, when there are enough of you… we can take down Rothgen."

The Nevadas and the people like them were

building their own army by using her kind. At least on this side, she could balance out the order of things.

"You're a valuable weapon against Rothgen. You're the evolution of the virus, and possibly of humanity. If we can't kill all the zombies, maybe there's a way we can make a vaccine out of your blood. As you learn more about yourself you'll be able to control the urges. Something good has to come of the end of the world and annihilation of our freedom."

Mr. Nevada looked away from Max and Nathan, opposite the city outline. He pulled out his binoculars and waved his hand in the air.

"It's them," Nathan said quietly. Max heard the sadness in his voice. They both knew goodbye was coming.

The trio stood on the rock formation as a group of four trekked down the opposite rocks. A dry creek bed lay in front of them as they crossed over.

Max saw that one of the group was taller than the rest. Everyone else was short like Max. Goggles covered their eyes, they wore long coats with hoods that covered their heads, and underneath they wore clothes similar to Max's.

She and the Nevadas started up the trail sloped toward the group. Mr. Nevada went ahead of the teenagers and walked up to the tallest person as they came up the rocks.

A girl pushed back her hood, revealing long brown hair that had been matted into little twist that fell down her back. A smile spread across her face and she hugged Mr. Nevada as though they were long-lost friends.

"It's my cousin, Evelyn," Nathan said. "Her mother didn't make it either, but she didn't die like mine did. She accidentally fed her milk to Evelyn before she turned. She's like you, just a little different because the virus didn't go through the placenta. Her mother's milk was tainted, but it was given to her at such a young age that she developed her own unique response."

"Wouldn't Rothgen want *her* so they can make a vaccine? Sounds like she would be a better candidate," Max said.

Mr. Nevada let go of Evelyn, and the other three

from the group came forward.

Nathan shook his head. "She's already been picked apart by Rothgen. They have her DNA on file. If they're going to use it, she doesn't need to be there. She's very resourceful. She escaped from the facility without any help from us. She came to our house, and Dad figured out how to get her out. Since then, we've been helping everyone we can."

Nathan took Max's hand and guided her toward his father and Evelyn. She looked healthier than any of the others.

As they approached, her smile widened. She looked happy to see Max, even though they didn't know each other.

"It's hard to believe you're going to give all this up to be like us again," Evelyn said.

"I have to do what's right for me and for everyone," Max said.

"I like you already. We are going to get you to a safe place tonight, and then in the morning, you'll be back to your old self. I brought a couple of friends in case we need anything," Evelyn said as she titled her head back in the direction of the other three.

They all pushed their hoods back. They were all boys. The guys walked closer, and Max felt a weird energy between all five of them. It threw her off-balance. Evelyn sensed the feeling.

"It's the virus emitting signals, searching out those who it has infected," she said. "It works with the zombies too. Unfortunately, it also means that we attract them, so it's not safe for us to stay here with my uncle and cousin. We need to go."

She pointed to Max's bag and the boys took it from her, even though she was sure that at her current strength, she could carry it more easily than them.

The boys and Evelyn started walking toward the slope they'd come up from. Evelyn hugged her uncle one more time as he threw candy bars to all four kids. Max turned around and looked at Nathan.

It was the last time she would see him. She was sure of it.

"Stop, you'll see me again," he said as he pulled her closer.

MAXINE

She smelled gunpowder, dirt, and a hint of her perfume from the night before. For a brief second, a thought of Ray passed through her. She hoped Rothgen wasn't cutting him apart limb by limb. She grasped tighter to Nathan's coat. Her natural instinct was to cling to the past and the life she'd known before.

"What if I don't?"

"If you don't? Then I know you are going to do everything you can to end Rothgen," Nathan said.

Maxine rested her head on Nathan's chest and closed her eyes. Tears rolled down her face.

A barrage of popping sounds came from nowhere, and Max felt something warm on the top of her head. When she looked up, she saw blood spewing from Nathan's mouth into her hair and upon her face.

"Nathan!" she screamed.

He whispered "Run," and shoved her away.

Maxine stumbled away from him. She heard the thump of his body hitting the ground. In front of her, four small bodies lay at odd angles, blood splattered everywhere. Bullets whizzed past her head, and they didn't stop, either; they came left and right. Maxine darted side to side, trying to outguess her attacker.

She skidded down the hill the kids had come up and dashed behind a large boulder. She heard rocks rolling down behind her. Then they stopped. Maxine's heart pounded in her ears.

"Miss Massachusetts, I don't want to hunt you down, but I will," her attacker threatened.

Maxine didn't dare look, but she had her suspicions that it was the Suit who'd been stalking her since the change had begun. The sun burned down on her pale face, and the boulder was hot against her back. It wouldn't be long before dehydration started.

She scanned the area: it was boulders, dirt, and the occasional pine tree disbursed in the low lands. It wasn't enough to cover her from being shot while trying to run away, and the backpack with all her supplies was at the top of the hill. She didn't know where she was at or where she was going.

Slowly shadows moved across the desert floor as Maxine sat in silence, running over her options.

Her attacker had not attempted to come down the hill. He must want her alive.

After a long deliberation, she pulled a pink handkerchief from her pocket. It was a souvenir from the night before. With great care, she scooted to the edge of the boulder, stuck her arm out and began to wave.

"I give up!"

Her voice echoed throughout the valley. The pink handkerchief waved in the air above her head as she walked into sight.

The Suit stared down at her through the scope of the gun. Maxine stood motionless.

"I figured you'd realize there was no way of getting out of this," the Suit said as he rested the gun by his side.

Back and forth they stared. Maxine started walking up the hill. It was difficult; she wasn't sure if it was dehydration or the start of her transforming back to a weakling.

"You know they lied to you," the Suit said. He chuckled lightly. "You don't get a choice. None of you do."

She stopped. *Great, the diabolical plan is revealed.*

"What do you mean?" she asked. If he wanted to prolong this, who was she to not play along with his need to feel superior?

"I *mean*, it isn't that you are going to turn into some little fat nobody again if you don't eat." He smiled. "You'll die."

Maxine gritted her teeth. The words came out like spit, "You're lying."

"No, I'm not. See those little shits laying over there?" the Suit said, pointing his gun at the children laying scattered a few feet from her "They're dead, right?"

She looked ahead. He was toying with her. She wasn't sure why he was doing it, but she wasn't going to fall for whatever he was trying to do.

"Just like like your shitty parents. You know, they didn't even try to fight. Your Mom—or Erin, I guess, since everyone knows she wasn't your real mother—was defiant, but that wimp of a dad, he fell like a tree at your front door," the Suit said, grinning wide.

Tears burned in Max's eyes. She couldn't explain why her parents had betrayed her, but she sure as hell didn't want to hear that they were dead.

"See? In the end, your parents knew they'd be dead out of this situation one way or another," the suit explained, with an arrogance about him.

Maxine started walking again, this time with more intensity. Every movement got her closer to him, and that was a chance to could rip his throat out.

"The Pennsylvania girl? She was just another pathetic, flesh-consuming zombie, like the rest of them in that morgue. Do you think her Daddy cares? Nope. Your hot-to-trot boyfriend, Ray? He's sitting pretty, because his ass *rolled* on you. That cute little med tech beat him into submission. She had her objectives from day one."

As Maxine hiked up the hill, it felt like the Suit was just running his mouth on and on. Her heart raced, and she tried to control her body's desire for water and flesh, and her personal need to kill the Suit as she reached the top.

It didn't surprise her that Ray had caved. He just

wasn't meant to be a rule-breaker; it had been beaten out of him a long time ago.

"Wasn't sure if you were going to make it up here," the Suit said, laughing. He had an ease and arrogance about him that wasn't seen often in McCarthy. He pointed the gun at Maxine. "You can get down on your knees now, and put your hands on top of your head."

The ground burned her knees as she crouched down. She placed her hands on her head and quietly assessed the situation.

It was obvious that Mr. Nevada was dead; half of his face was gone. Nathan lay on his back. She could have been imagining it, but it looked like his chest slowly and unevenly rose and fell. If nothing else, the Suit had gotten a lung for sure.

He walked over to her and grabbed her right hand, squeezing it tight. He jerked her arm behind her.

"Ow! You're hurting me!" Maxine protested.

"You're lucky I don't put a bullet in your head, little girl. Aren't you gonna get mad and rip me apart when you don't get your way?" he taunted.

"You'd like that, wouldn't you? If I turned into a monster? It'd give you a reason to kill me." It started to make sense why he'd told her all those horrible things.

"Yeah, it would. I'd kill you with a clear conscience, and Rothgen couldn't say a thing about it." The Suit grabbed her left hand and pulled it behind her back as well, binding her hands together. Out of nowhere, he smacked her upside the head.

"Poor Maxine Mess-a-shit-etts, always a freak, disgusting no matter what you look like." He hit her again.

"You know what you can do?" she yelled. "Go fuck yourself!"

"Do you even know what that means?" He hit her again. "You stupid little girl, trying to use the big bad words that Mommy and Daddy weren't allowed to say."

Blow by blow, Maxine felt the rage inside of her increase. She fell to the ground after he went from smacking to punching her in the face. She stared over at Nathan and closed her eyes, wishing he was

326

near her.

The Suit flopped down on Maxine. His weight felt like it would crush her chest. She felt the blows, one after another as he began to weep.

"You little pieces of garbage took everything from me. *Everything.*" The punches continued, but she felt more than blood streaming down her face. He'd must've started spitting as well as crying in his rage. Over and over, she imagined it in her mind's eye, Nathan's dead body rising to rescue her before the Suit beat her to death. She held her breath. This was the one time she needed to turn into her alter self and it wasn't working.

The beating abruptly stopped. The Suit rolled off of her. She looked up to see Nathan chewing on his neck.

"Typical," the Suit said, and pulled his handgun from his side.

He shot Nathan in the head—three consecutive pops. Nathan started falling after the first, but the Suit kept firing.

Tears stopped rolling down Maxine's face. The rage was full upon her. She busted the ties binding her hands and pushed herself up, grabbing the gun from the Suit. There were no words now, only flesh.

Instinctually, she began where Nathan had left off and ripped through the warm, pulsing flesh. The Suit screamed and screamed. It was music to her ears. She kept eating until she blacked out.

It was morning when Maxine awoke. Her clothes were crusted over with blood. She got up and looked to her right. The Suit had no throat or shoulders. In her rage, she'd flayed him apart with her bare hands.

Shockingly, she didn't want to throw up. She pushed herself up, feeling stronger than ever. In the truck were several jugs of water. She jumped in the back, pulled out one of the jugs and chugged as though it were the last water on Earth. She poured the rest over her head.

There were more clean clothes, so she grabbed a new shirt and pants, slipped them on, and then jumped out of the semi-truck.

Nathan Nevada's body lay over by the Suit. She

walked over and stared at him. Had she willed him to her? How had Nathan become a zombie if he didn't have the infection? Were any of the rules she'd been told about the virus true?

There were so many questions, but the truth was they wouldn't be answered if she went back to McCarthy. Besides--if her parents were dead, did she *want* to go back?

She leaned down and kissed Nathan on his lips. He was cold, but there was no worry of her infecting him now. She cried until she was heaving so hard that she vomited. Maxine remembered what was in her stomach, and she cried some more.

The bodies were strewn around the area still in the spots where death claimed them. For a moment, she thought about burning their bodies so Rothgen couldn't use them, but the Nevadas would have wanted her to get away from the scene as soon as possible. Rothgen could come retrieve what was left. She didn't care.

She looked at the map and compass from her backpack. Phoenix was the most logical choice, as it was closest. Her instincts told her that Rothgen would look there for her first.

She scanned the map, looking for a large area where she could hide out. Las Vegas looked good, and Mr. Nevada had lived there before the war. She pointed the compass west, picked up the backpack, and started walking.

The story will continue in

MAD MAXINE

Acknowledgements

My Love

Timothy W. Long, I thank you for always being the guy who assured me that my bicycle would make it off the ramp, fly over the ravine, and land successfully. I met you in 2010 and over the years we developed a great friendship. Now, every day that I get to roll over and look at your smiling face I feel so grateful. Thanks for being in my life. I love you.

Family

I would like to thank my mother, Martha. There are many portions of this book that are loosely based on my struggle with Polycystic Ovarian Syndrome during puberty. We had no clue what was wrong with me. I was not a normal girl personality wise and the fact that my body wouldn't cooperate made it worse. Which leads me to thank her for encouraging me to check out the following book from the library: Betty Cornell's *Teenage Popularity Guide* because the book has always stuck with me. Thanks for letting me cry on your lap when I would come home from school lonely, hurt, and feeling lower than dirt. I love you.

Out of all the people in the world who've always made me feel normal, my sister is that person. Jennifer, thank you for not laughing me out of writing. I appreciate your patience, acceptance, and friendship. Being placed on this planet with a sister like you is a blessing. Also, your courage to be a weirdo and hold your head up in high school is something I still think about with pride.

And, of course, I can't leave out my brother, Larry. Thanks for always looking up to me, I still don't know why you ever have, but it keeps me trying to be a good big sister. It is still funny that out of the three of us you are the only one that was a stereotypical teenager, you jock.

Also, thank you, uncle Merrill, who encouraged all of us to create stories before we could put them on paper through dioramas and staging plays. To all my other family members, I love you all and appreciate your support.

The final person that must absolutely be acknowledged is my grandmother, Mary. She was the 1950s teenager, and if she hadn't been such an excellent storyteller, I don't know that this world would have materialized.

My Creative Friends

There are so many of you! I don't want any hurt feelings so I'll leave it at this, you know who you are and that I'm ever so grateful for your faith in me.

About the Author

Katie Cord lives in the Pacific Northwest with her three mix-mash dogs, a Bengal cat, and a million books. She is a nurse, writer and publisher. She loves science fiction, post-apocalyptic, dystopian, horror, and dark humor stories. When she isn't doing all the things, she loves to spend time with her boyfriend, Timothy W. Long, power watching Netflix and trying to take over the world.

You can find her at:

www.katiecord.com

www.evilgirlfriendmedia.com.

Unsure of what to read next?

Pick up *He Left Her to the Altar, She Left Him to the Zombies here:* http://bit.ly/HeLeftHerSheLeftZombies

When you're done, take a look at the Evil Girlfriend Media Catalogue here:
http://www.evilgirlfriendmedia.com/

Made in the USA
Middletown, DE
28 April 2023

29366798R00205